W9-BLD-607

I sit on the floor and start to draw a dandelion pushing its way up on one of the cards. Behind it, I draw the sun rising over a mountain. And the sky is beautiful. I add orange and red and yellow all mixing together. And then I add glitter glue all over it.

I close my eyes tight and imagine Mrs. DeSouza looking over my shoulder. "Look at that light. Look at that sparkle," she'd say in her beautiful Jamaican accent. "And think about it, Libby, that's happening every day in every part of the world. Isn't that amazing?"

I open my eyes. In the shadow of the mountain, I write the word *amazing*.

I stare at it, then I add two more words.

You are
amazing

Because if I am going to have to sit in this room for a month, this is what I need staring at me.

ALSO BY ANN BRADEN

The Benefits of Being an Octopus

FLiGHT
OF THE
PUFFiN

ANN BRADEN

Nancy Paulsen Books

NANCY PAULSEN BOOKS
An imprint of Penguin Random House LLC, New York

First published in the United States of America by Nancy Paulsen Books,
an imprint of Penguin Random House LLC, 2021
First paperback edition published 2022

Copyright © 2021 by Ann Braden

Penguin supports copyright. Copyright fuels creativity, encourages diverse voices,
promotes free speech, and creates a vibrant culture. Thank you for buying an authorized
edition of this book and for complying with copyright laws by not reproducing, scanning,
or distributing any part of it in any form without permission. You are supporting writers
and allowing Penguin to continue to publish books for every reader.

Nancy Paulsen Books & colophon are trademarks of Penguin Random House LLC.
Penguin Books & colophon are registered trademarks of Penguin Books Limited.

Visit us online at penguinrandomhouse.com

THE LIBRARY OF CONGRESS HAS CATALOGED THE HARDCOVER EDITION AS FOLLOWS:
Names: Braden, Ann, author.
Title: Flight of the puffin / Ann Braden.
Description: New York: Nancy Paulsen Books, an imprint of Penguin Random House, [2021]
Summary: Told in multiple voices, seventh-grader Libby sets off a chain of events that
brings hope and encouragement to four different individuals across the country who are
dealing with bullies, acceptance, homelessness, and grief.
Identifiers: LCCN 2021003044 | ISBN 9781984816061 (hardcover) |
ISBN 9781984816078 (ebook)
Subjects: CYAC: Encouragement—Fiction. | Self-acceptance—Fiction. |
Bullying—Fiction. | Homeless persons—Fiction. | Gender identity—Fiction.
Classification: LCC PZ7.1.B7267 Fl 2021 | DDC [Fic]—dc23
LC record available at https://lccn.loc.gov/2021003044

Printed in the United States of America

ISBN 9781984816085

1st Printing

LSCH

Design by Suki Boynton
Text set in Chaparral Pro

This book is a work of fiction. Any references to historical events,
real people, or real places are used fictitiously. Other names, characters, places,
and events are products of the author's imagination, and any resemblance to
actual events or places or persons, living or dead, is entirely coincidental.

The publisher does not have any control over and does not assume any
responsibility for author or third-party websites or their content.

For Ethan and Alice
May you fly free

LIBBY

MONDAY, APRIL 30

THIS IS GOING to be the best sunrise ever. I slather on more orange paint, catching the drips with my paintbrush and mixing them into the hot pink. I swirl it around and around. My paintbrush is like the band teacher conducting. I don't play an instrument, but I've seen him waving his arms when I peek in the band room.

I dip my brush back into the can and make even bigger circles, then add extra dollops above, like sparks flying up. I love how the sparks look. I know that's not how people usually make sunrises, but there's fire involved, right? I add more on the other side. I have to. There's too much joy inside me to not.

I step back. I knew this would make me feel better!

Now it's time to add the yellow. I kneel down and pry the lid off the can. A blazing inferno just waiting to be unleashed.

That's when I hear footsteps.

And Principal Hecton's voice.

"Libby Delmar, what have you done to that wall?"

I sit in the seat in front of Principal Hecton's desk. He collapses into his chair and lets out a sigh.

His desk would look better with polka dots. He could get the magnetic kind, and then those of us having to stare at it could rearrange them to keep it fresh. Orange, blue, and purple dots would be nice.

Principal Hecton leans back and closes his eyes. "I should have known."

Maybe with a few yellow dots. That'd really pop.

He opens his eyes and leans over the desk. "Are you going to be just like your brother? And your dad?"

No way! Is he kidding? I try to do the exact opposite of them.

"Because I don't think I can handle that," he says.

Okay, maybe I did do some bad stuff . . . but it was to make things better. And it already did. I eye the still-wet paint splotches on my green pants. Value added!

"And don't think I didn't hear the stories about your grandpa, too, back when I was in school." Principal Hecton shakes his head. "I've got to tell you, I'm tired of your family pushing people around."

I press my lips together and try to imagine that sunrise. I'm not like them.

Principal Hecton eyes me. "And weren't you just in my office a week ago?"

It was twelve days.

"For physically assaulting Danielle Fisher."

That was a mistake. I shouldn't have let her get to me. I wasn't wearing that awesome rainbow outfit for other people. I was wearing it for myself. Who cares if she said I looked like a freaky clown.

Well, my fist cared.

"As you know, we have rules around here for a reason . . ."

He keeps talking, and I have to bite my lip hard so I don't talk back. Yes, I know punching her in the face was the wrong thing to do. Yes, I know that "not thinking was the problem," but did Danielle think before *she* talked? Because if she did, that's even worse.

And I get that girls aren't supposed to give other people bloody noses. Instead, everyone should be like model student Danielle, who fights the "right" way: by convincing the entire softball team to stop talking to me. So that even Adrianna Randell now walks past me without a word, as if we haven't spent nights sprawled on pillows and giggling on her bedroom floor.

That sunrise was going to help me ignore it all.

Principal Hecton is squeezing his hands together and

almost whispering. "I'm going to have to do it," he mutters.

Is he talking to himself?

"Okay," he says louder, and lets out a long sigh. "I am going to call your father. And tell him he needs to come to school. He needs to see for himself what you've done."

My dad. Really? I've never seen him in my school. He's not the kind to come to open house or parent conferences. It doesn't matter how many times teachers call home to schedule a conversation about my missing work or my "inattentiveness in class." He doesn't exactly appreciate getting "advice" about his children.

"I'm not like my family," I blurt out.

Principal Hecton laughs nervously. "I wish that were true." He starts writing up an in-school suspension slip. "Right now, I want you to bring those cans of paint back to the art closet and clean up that closet while you're there. Then tomorrow, during your in-school suspension, you'll be repainting that wall white again, like it's supposed to be."

Mrs. Ecker, the long-term art sub, is waiting for me when I get to the art room. She leads me toward the art supply closet as if I don't know where it is. As if I wasn't just in there an hour ago, when the door was left open like an invitation and the paint cans were screaming to me. I used to get to go in the closet all the time when Mrs. DeSouza was still here and we had an actual art teacher.

I carry the paint cans into the closet and breathe in. It smells glorious. Of course, not as good as when Mrs. DeSouza would bring lunch from her brother's Jamaican food truck and the room would smell like jerk chicken and paint. Those lunch periods were heaven, and I thought I had it made.

"Chop-chop," Mrs. Ecker says. "There's plenty to do." She pokes at a pile of paint tubes missing their caps and recoils like a rainbow slug just slimed her.

I set down the cans of paint and look around. So many art supplies. Just sitting here!

"When I was in school, we would respect the property of our superiors," Mrs. Ecker says. "What would your parents think? You should listen to them."

If I listened to what my dad said, I would have punched Danielle Fisher long ago. I run my fingers along the bottles of acrylic paints. And then I remember I'm supposed to be cleaning, so I nudge them until they're in a bit of a line. Paints shouldn't sit unused like this. It makes me twitchy.

I move on to a different shelf. There are a whole lot of sheets of little ceramic tiles that Mrs. DeSouza ordered for a mosaic before she moved away from Spring Falls. Some have slipped out of place, and I start to restack them, but there's something else jammed in the way. I move a few of them to the side and see the smooth rock Mrs. DeSouza used to keep on her desk. She left so suddenly that she must have forgotten it. I turn it over in my hand. Carved in a circle along the edge are the words *Create the world of your dreams*.

Here is someone who got me.

But is that even possible? Because the world of my dreams would have a sunrise opposite the girls' locker room that *doesn't* have to get painted over.

I glance at Mrs. Ecker. She's studying the fire escape map on the wall. As quick as I can, I shove the rock into the pocket of my hoodie.

Because what if what the rock says is possible? I mean, Mrs. DeSouza was someone who knew what she was talking about. Like, she knew how to draw a bird with only four lines.

Before Mrs. Ecker looks back at me, I swipe a bottle of glitter glue too. Because glitter.

That's when the secretary's voice comes on the art-room intercom. "Mrs. Ecker? Libby Delmar's father is here. Please send her to the office."

I can't believe my dad is here. I walk as slowly as possible down the hall, wondering how mad he'll be. And it's not exactly predictable who he'll be mad at. The only constant in life is that it's never at my older brother, Rex. He might have gotten suspended all the time when he was in school, but as long as Rex won the fight, my dad didn't care.

I feel the glitter glue in my hoodie pocket and stop. I'm

pretty sure the world of my dreams would be all kinds of sparkly. I glance in both directions down the hallway. Empty.

I take out the glitter glue and squeeze a dollop of it onto one of the drab hallway tiles. I kneel down and spread it all around, hoping it'll look like the ocean waves reflecting that sunrise.

Except that when I stand up, it only looks like a smear. A sad gray smear.

Who am I kidding? My world is too much of a mess to just add sparkle.

The sound of footsteps coming gets me walking again, and I practice my excuse in my head: *I'm just on my way to the office.*

But it's not a teacher who comes around the corner— it's a boy from my English class.

"Mr. Cruck told me to find you to give you this stuff," he says. "We're starting five-paragraph essays, and we're supposed to color-code our notes, and he wants you to . . ."

He keeps talking, but all I can see are the index cards and the box of colored pencils that he's handing me like a gift. Wasting these on a five-paragraph essay? No chance.

A five-paragraph essay is not the world of my dreams.

ᥫᩣ

When I get to the office, my dad is yelling at Principal Hecton. "I'm in the middle of running a business! You think I have time to come here and help you do your job, Paulie?"

Paulie? Who's Paulie?

And then I realize: Principal Paul Hecton. I suddenly have a vague recollection that my dad and the principal were in school together.

Principal Hecton certainly looks like he remembers—and I bet he's having a whole lot of regret right now.

"I'd like you to see the vandalism before it gets painted over," he says.

"Then take a picture of it," my dad says. "You heard of a camera?"

Maybe my dad isn't angry with me, but this isn't much better. I take a step back and try to merge with the leafy potted plant at the entrance to the main office. Through the glass wall, I see none other than Danielle Fisher walking by. Great. Now the whole seventh grade will hear about this.

"You just want to make yourself feel important with all your calling home and handing out suspension slips," my dad continues. "But if you think you can use my daughter in your power games, you've got another thing coming."

Principal Hecton's face reddens. He picks up a student handbook. "With all due respect, I'd like to refer you to page thirty-four, where it discusses the vandalizing of school property. There is nothing personal about—"

"Libby, get your stuff," my dad says, turning to me. "We're leaving."

I look between my dad and Principal Hecton. "Right now?"

"I'm not spending another minute being talked down to by someone who didn't even know how to tie his shoes until fourth grade."

⁓

I keep my backpack perched on my lap for the drive home. We live just on the other side of downtown, and my dad doesn't exactly drive slowly, but still, it's a long eight minutes.

The radio guy is yammering on about the varsity boys' baseball game last night. My dad turns it way up, as a not so subtle jab at me. He hates it that I'm off the softball team, but who in their right mind would stay on a team that doesn't want them?

We pull into the driveway, and I'm about to get out when my dad relocks the doors.

"You're grounded," he says. "For a month."

A month? Is he serious?

Then he unlocks the car and climbs out. "And don't embarrass me again."

By the time I've steadied my breath, my dad is already at the bottom of our driveway talking with our neighbor Hal—probably convincing him to let him tune up his lawn mower.

Our apartment is in one of those big sprawling houses built when the mills in town were chugging away. And even though the house has four apartments, somehow my dad got our landlord to give him full use of the garage for his engine business. Plus, with him strutting up and down the driveway all the time, the other renters decided to not even try to use the two parking spots in front of it. They just park on the street.

Last year, in sixth grade, we learned how there are tons of crowded old mill towns like ours on riverbanks up and down the East Coast. Maybe they're all sports-obsessed, and maybe every single one has a guy like my dad, who, no matter what happens, makes everything about him.

I push open the passenger door. In a crack of the driveway, a dandelion is poking through, and I focus on it, keeping my head down.

I go straight inside to the kitchen. At least there's a new box of that healthy cereal in the cupboard—my mom actually listened when I told her what I'd learned about the importance of whole grains. I reach in the fridge to get some milk, and there's a whole chicken defrosting in there. My mom's currently on a seventy-six-ways-to-make-chicken kick.

Part of me wants to call her. But only a small part, because she hasn't forgiven me for quitting the softball team either. And my mom doesn't exactly let things go. You should see the way she stands at the checkout counter in the 7-Eleven and stares down the kids who try to shoplift. She doesn't let up until they've dropped whatever they were holding and run away. And she's been looking at me like that for the past twelve days.

When I get to my bedroom, I throw my backpack onto the floor. Smack in the middle of the floor, too, because this whole room should be mine. But even though my brother, Rex, works at L&H Wholesalers and has an apartment of his own, he still uses this room as his closet. He never got over having to share it. When an unexpected baby sister shows up when you're eight, she'll always be unwelcome.

At least he doesn't sleep here. I remember Rex lying on his bed, zinging baseballs at the ceiling on the days he was suspended. The cracks in the paint are still up there.

I'm not like Rex, am I?

Even if I'm surrounded by his stuff. Even if we come from the same parents. Even if I just got suspended for vandalism.

I squeeze my eyes shut and press my fists to my forehead.

I.

Will.

Not.

Be.

Like.

Them.

I open my eyes and kick my backpack clear across the

room. It lands upside down on my bed, spilling out some contents. And suddenly, I remember what's inside it. I scramble over to my bed and carefully take stock: three index cards, five colored pencils, one bottle of glitter glue, and one rock. *Create the world of your dreams.*

How exactly am I supposed to create the world of my dreams with just this?

But then I remember what Mrs. DeSouza used to say to me when I'd stare at a blank white sheet of paper. *One line is all it takes.*

I think of that dandelion pushing its way through the crack in the driveway. That's me. That is *me*. I just have to find my way to the sunshine.

And these are the materials I have.

I sit on the floor and start to draw a dandelion pushing its way up on one of the cards. Behind it, I draw the sun rising over a mountain. And the sky is beautiful. I add orange and red and yellow all mixing together. And then I add glitter glue all over it.

I close my eyes tight and imagine Mrs. DeSouza looking over my shoulder. "Look at that light. Look at that sparkle," she'd say in her beautiful Jamaican accent. "And think about it, Libby, that's happening every day in every part of the world. Isn't that amazing?"

I open my eyes. In the shadow of the mountain, I write the word *amazing*.

I stare at it, then I add two more words.

You are
amazing

Because if I am going to have to sit in this room for a month, this is what I need staring at me.

JACK
MONDAY, APRIL 30

JOEY IS TUGGING my shirt again. "Jack," he says.

I stop dribbling the ball and squat down next to him on the blacktop so I can hear him over the shrieks of the other little kids. "What's up, little man?"

He points. Up. "Two more points."

Joey doesn't say many words when he's focused on something.

I put the basketball in his hands. "You ready?"

He grins. He's ready.

I spin him around so he's facing away from me, and I lift him toward the rim. "Here comes Joey for the dunk," I yell.

I can feel Joey's ribs through his shirt as he squeals and tips the ball into the hoop. He's the same size my little brother, Alex, was. And just as focused.

I set him back down on the blacktop, and he runs after

the ball. I know he's going to want to go again. The black-top is finally clear of snow, and he's determined to get to ten points this recess. I glance at Todd and Sturgis, who are waiting for me to come play football, but they'll have to wait a little longer.

A speck on the blacktop glints in the sun, like glitter. I stoop down, but it's only a piece of neon-green foam. Probably from the playground ball that's starting to fall apart. I flick it off my finger and swallow hard. Alex used to sneak baggies of glitter home from school in his lunch box. He loved that stuff, but my parents didn't. "No boy needs glitter," my dad said. "It's just going to get everywhere," my mom said.

And it did. Scattered in his bedroom rug, tucked in the folds of the back seat of our pickup, in the corners of Alex's kindergarten cubby. I was still finding that glitter long after he was gone.

He's at my shirt again. Joey, that is. He tugs at it even though I'm already looking right at him. His eyes are lit up. Like inside him a whole stadium full of people is chanting his name, hoping he can deliver the game-winning dunk.

"One more time, okay?" I say.

When I cross the blacktop to where Sturgis and Todd are waiting, Sturgis tosses the football to me. "Took you long enough."

I shrug and throw it back to him. "You could have started without me."

"Not if we want to play three-on-three."

I look across the muddy field to where the three other kids are waiting. "Come on. They're sixth graders. You could've taken them."

Our school has three boys in sixth grade and the three of us in seventh. There once was a guy in the grade above us, but he moved to a "less rural" part of Vermont back in third grade. But the sixth graders are cool enough. When you're in a two-room K–8 schoolhouse, you find a way to get along with everyone.

"You want to play or not?" Sturgis says.

"Yeah, I want to." I grab the ball out of his hand and take off across the field at top speed so Sturgis and Todd don't have a chance of catching me.

I team up with two of the sixth graders, and our team is up 14–3 when Mr. Sasko gives his nod from the door to let me know that recess is over. I stuff the football under my arm and call to the rest of the kids to head in. This afternoon, I'm supposed to read to the younger kids—probably *Cloudy With a Chance of Meatballs* again if Mrs. Lincoln lets the kids choose.

I'm rounding up the last of the younger students when an unfamiliar car pulls into the parking space next to Mr. Sasko's truck. It's shiny. Like it didn't just spend all of mud season on Haycock's dirt roads. The woman who gets out of the car has on a suit and high heels—not the best footwear for our muddy parking lot.

I'm about to follow the other kids inside when Mr. Sasko appears at the door again. His face is strained.

He strides out to meet the woman. "Lucinda, it's good to see you. I don't think I've ever seen you outside of Montpelier. Welcome to Haycock School. To what do we owe this special visit?"

The lady gives a tight smile. "Oh, I'm just coming to check things out and see what you're up to at your little school."

"What we're up to?" He chuckles and motions me over to them. "Well then, you can see the high quality of students we develop."

I walk over and stand tall next to Mr. Sasko.

He puts his hand on my shoulder. "Jack, I'd like to introduce you to Ms. Duxbury. She works for Vermont's Agency of Education. This is Jack Galenos. You won't find a finer student anywhere."

"It's a pleasure to meet you," I say. I do my best to give her a good, firm handshake.

"Jack, while I get the older students started on this afternoon's lesson, would you give Ms. Duxbury a tour of our school?"

I swallow. "I'd be honored."

Mr. Sasko squeezes my shoulder. "You're in good hands, Ms. Duxbury."

Ms. Duxbury nods to me. "Let's get started, then."

Mr. Sasko disappears inside, and I'm left with Ms. Suit in the parking lot.

"Well, this is our play area," I say, gesturing to the slide, the swings, and the sandbox. "And our field."

"I see," she says. "And what sorts of activities do you do out here?"

She's looking at the creaky set of swings like they might collapse at any moment. Even though they won't. I've seen Mr. Sasko swing next to a kid who's been having a hard day, and those swings are strong.

"Swing," I say. "Play in the sand." Isn't it obvious? If I add *Go down the slide*, will she think I'm being a smart aleck? "Play football," I say instead.

She nods and writes something in her notebook.

When she's done, she walks over to the swing set. "So just dirt underneath this?"

"The grass gets worn away," I say.

"But no wood chips?"

Does it look like there are wood chips? Does she really need me to tell her that?

But she's looking at me like she does.

"No wood chips," I say.

She writes that down in her notebook.

"How about I show you the inside?" I say.

She nods. "Please do."

I try to walk slowly so she doesn't have to move too fast. Where could those shoes possibly make sense?

I hold the door open for her, and I'm happy to see everything inside is in order. Mrs. Lincoln has all of the youngers

gathered around her while she reads—you guessed it—
Cloudy With a Chance of Meatballs, and in the far room Mr.
Sasko is working with the olders.

I point to the back wall, where there's a huge painting
of the hilly farms of Haycock with our schoolhouse in the
center. "Mr. Sasko designed that mural, and we all helped
paint it."

Ms. Duxbury nods. But that was a good nod, right?

"At the beginning of each day, we all gather in here, and
Mrs. Lincoln plays 'God Bless America.'" I nod toward the
guitar in the corner.

Ms. Duxbury makes a few more notes, and I wait near
the guitar. When I came back to school after the summer we
lost Alex, Mrs. Lincoln played "On the Loose" and everyone
sang along. I still don't know how they found out that was
Alex's favorite song. Mrs. Lincoln said she knew the song
from when she was a Girl Scout, but I don't know when
the rest of them found time to learn it. I just know that
those four minutes of singing were what got me through
that year.

I'm not about to tell Ms. Duxbury any of that, though.

"How many students are in this school right now?"
she asks.

"Seventeen," I say.

"Two teachers for seventeen students?"

"Well, yeah," I say. "Because of course we have to divide
up sometimes." No way are the little kids going to sit

through a lesson on ratios. Does she actually expect that to work?

But she's writing in her notebook again *and* raising her eyebrows at the same time.

"Let me show you the other room," I say.

"There's only one other room?"

"Well, there are the bathrooms too."

"Would you show them to me?"

"Uh, sure." I lead her out into the tiny hall that runs between the two main rooms and stop in front of the bathroom doors. Why does she want to see them? All there is in each one is a toilet and a sink. Is she going to go into the boys' room?

But when I turn back, I realize that she doesn't want to go inside them. She's just scribbling in that stupid notebook again.

"Is there a separate bathroom for the teachers?"

I try not to sigh. "No. They use these."

"So, no gender-neutral bathroom?"

I'm not even sure what that is, but I know we don't have one. I glance in at Mr. Sasko, and he catches my eye and comes out into the hallway. I guess my face didn't communicate the cool and calm I was going for.

"How's the tour going? Is Jack being a gentleman?" Mr. Sasko jokes. Because of course I'm being a gentleman. I always am.

But Ms. Duxbury doesn't smile. "It's very useful for me to be here." She pulls a folder from her bag and hands it to Mr. Sasko. "I'm sure you're already aware of the recent guidelines the Agency of Education has released."

Mr. Sasko nods as he takes the folder. "You all are working hard, aren't you?"

"Just trying to make sure our limited grant funds are going to the right schools."

"Well, those Small School Grants are important to us. And we are always open to suggestions for making our school better," Mr. Sasko says. "Like last year, Jack had the great idea to get us outside for a whole day every month. Next month, we'll be launching bottle rockets." He puts his hand on my shoulder. "The students are planning it themselves. Isn't that right, Jack?"

I nod. "We're trying to find the trajectory that'll land a rocket in Mrs. Drake's old pig trough."

Mr. Sasko laughs. "I promised the winner all-you-can-eat bacon."

"I beg your pardon, Mr. Sasko, but this is not a joke." Ms. Duxbury taps her notebook. "I wouldn't treat the directives from the Agency of Education simply as 'suggestions.' The only schools that receive grants will be those who can demonstrate academic excellence, operational efficiency, and compliance with Agency of Education standards."

Mr. Sasko stiffens and takes his hand off my shoulder.

"Jack, how about you see if Mrs. Lincoln needs help with the youngers." He turns to Ms. Duxbury. "Why don't we continue this conversation in my office?"

"It was a pleasure to meet you," I lie.

Ms. Duxbury nods, but she doesn't even look at me. Instead, she disappears with Mr. Sasko into the oversized closet he and Mrs. Lincoln use as an office.

I slip into the back of the youngers' room. At the moment, I'm really hoping some meatballs will fall from the sky. And that one will splat right on top of Ms. Duxbury's notebook.

My dad always told me that the beauty of living in the middle of nowhere was that we get to make our own decisions about what's right for us. I eye that lady's shiny car through the window—there's no way she knows what we need better than we do.

VINCENT

MONDAY, APRIL 30

I SETTLE ONTO the floor behind the locker-room trash can with my math notebook. Only a few more weeks until we get to the geometry unit. I've been teaching myself geometry online, but it's not the same as having Mr. Bond explain it.

I turn to a fresh page in my notebook and start drawing triangles. Triangles are everywhere you look. There are triangles in the floor tiles, in the metal supports beneath the locker-room benches—even the people in this school form a triangle. One side is the popular kids, who are good at PE and looking cool. Another side is the kids who want to be like the popular kids but aren't quite as good at that stuff. And the third side is the creative, artistic kids, who don't care about being popular and are instead cool in their non-popularity. Everyone knows where they fit.

My mom wants me to be one of those creative kids.

She runs an art supply store where we live in Seattle, and she's got short purple hair. She even named me Vincent after that *Starry Night* artist guy, van Gogh. But I didn't get those genes. I guess when my mom was looking through the sperm donors' profiles, she didn't think she'd need to choose someone artistic. She thought she'd have that part covered. She was wrong.

The other kids at school form a triangle. But me? I am a point in space.

I finish filling up one page with triangles and begin a new page. Suddenly, there's a sneaker next to my math book. Two sneakers. With legs.

"You want us to believe you were actually on a baseball team?"

It's Cal Carpenter. And a bunch of his friends. He's talking to me, isn't he?

"What team?" I say.

He gestures at my shirt with his foot. I look down and remember I'm wearing an old rec league baseball shirt. I made contact with the ball precisely one time. That was when a fly ball from my own teammate hit me on the head while I was sitting on the bench. And there was no "making the team." There was only my mom "making me do it."

"When's that shirt from? Third grade?"

"Fourth," I say. Which is totally different from third. I can't be the only seventh grader who still fits into shirts from fourth grade.

"That's sad," Cal says to his friends. "I bet he hasn't been able to be on a team since then."

He doesn't actually sound sad about it.

I am also not sad about not being on a baseball team. They announced baseball tryouts a few weeks ago. All I could think was, there's no way anyone could convince me to play that horrible sport again.

"Look," Cal's friend Zachary says, "he's even drawing baseball diamonds in his notebook!"

"It's his dream, isn't it? To be on a baseball team again!" Cal says. "His dream!"

Cal and Zachary and the rest of them start laughing all over themselves.

"I don't care about baseball," I say.

"Sure you don't," Cal says.

"That's why you're drawing fields in your notebook!" yells Zachary.

"They're triangles," I say.

"Triangles!" Now they're doubled over in laughter. "Right."

Why do they care if I like baseball? Is it not possible to mind your own business at this school?

They're still laughing when they pick me up and put me in an empty locker, like it's the easiest thing in the world, never mind my flailing limbs.

The sound of a slamming metal door is loud when you're outside a locker, but it's even louder when you're inside.

And inside it's a tight fit, too, even for a seventh grader who still fits into fourth-grade shirts. I guess the makers of the locker might have known this would happen too. Why else would they add air vents? But then why didn't they add a way to open the door from the inside?

I squirm a little.

Nope. Not happening.

Just pretend you're in your room at home. And you're just choosing not to move.

I close my eyes and picture the poster I have on my wall of Katherine Johnson. It's of the real one, not the actress who played her in the movie *Hidden Figures*, even though that was how I found out about her. "It has rockets," my mom said when she took me to see the movie. What my mom didn't tell me is that it was about three Black women mathematicians who kept having doors shut on them but found ways to open them because they could do all these complicated calculations in their head. Like math was their superpower. What would Katherine Johnson do right now?

I open my eyes. She would find triangles. She could see triangles everywhere she looked.

I peer through the slits in the locker. I can still see the triangles on the floor tiles. I start counting them.

When I spot Ms. Lemmick, the PE teacher, I bang on the locker like my life depends on it.

When she opens the locker door and I fall out, she looks

me up and down and then shakes her head. "You're missing fourth period, Vincent."

Right. As though I purposely chose to hang out in a small, smelly locker.

She basically has the same expression as in PE class when she's just yelled at me to run. Because in her mind, my version of "running," which is a mix of stumbling forward and walking quickly, does not count.

"Yeah," I mumble. "Thanks."

She sighs and pulls a stack of hall passes from her hoodie pocket. "Here. I'll write you a pass."

"Thanks," I say again as I take it from her.

"Do you want to report who did this?"

I shake my head and turn to go. Why do I feel like all of this is my fault?

"You've got to toughen up," she calls after me. "Otherwise, they'll destroy you."

Thanks a lot.

My mom's at the kitchen table when I get home to our apartment. Monday afternoon is the one time during the week she doesn't work. It's her "serendipitous time." She's got an enormous collection of colored pens organized in glass jars all around her.

I hang up my raincoat to dry. By spring in Seattle, it doesn't rain as often as in the winter, but it still rains.

Today the barometric pressure is 29.46 and holding steady. No sun coming out anytime soon.

"How was your day?" she asks.

"Fine."

"What was the most interesting part?"

"None of it."

"That's not true." She stands up and puts her finger on my nose. "It was your day, and you are exceedingly interesting, and therefore any day of yours is interesting to me."

I shake my head.

"Hey! Check out what I found for you at Second Chance." She runs over to her bag and pulls out a T-shirt with a sloth riding a motorcycle. "Isn't it funny? Like how they're so slow, but not if they're on a motorcycle. Mind-blowing, right?"

I nod and try to laugh.

She hands me the shirt. "Wear it tomorrow. It'll crack people up."

I look at the garden of flowers she's been sketching in her notebook. Purple with stripes of blue, orange, and pink. "What kind of flowers are those?"

"They're from my imagination."

"So, not real."

She wraps her arm around me. "Who knows? Might be a not-yet-discovered flower. It's a great big world out there."

I nod. "I'm going to go do my homework."

"Are you sure?" She squeezes me tighter. "You just got out of school. Give yourself time to be creative. Go exploring."

"Mom...I..."

"This is why I wish we could have a dog. You'd be heading out on a long walk together right now."

"I just walked home from school. In the rain. I don't need to go for another walk."

"You could be about to discover things you've never discovered. Going on adventures."

"That's just in books. Real dogs don't go on adventures. They just go poop."

Also, I'm terrified of dogs. They bark, and there's the whole slobber thing. Thank goodness my mom is allergic.

She holds up her notebook. "Okay. Want to color these flowers with me instead? I got a new set of markers you could test out."

"Mom."

She sighs. "Fine. But at least get yourself a snack first. Math is bad enough when you're not calorie-deprived."

I bring some carrots and hummus into my room, drop the motorcycling-sloth shirt on the floor, and sit underneath my poster of Katherine Johnson. It's a giant picture of Katherine when she was a kid, and she's got her hands on her hips, looking up like she can do anything. It says REACHING FOR THE MOON across the top, because that's the title of Katherine's autobiography. I begged my mom's bookstore friend to let me have the poster after the event at her store was over.

I take a bite of a carrot and glare at the shirt. No matter how hard I try, I can't be the cool, creative kid my mom wants me to be. And I sure don't want to play baseball like Cal Carpenter said either.

I jab a carrot into the container of hummus and try to get the vision of Cal Carpenter's face out of my head. I need to have some sort of signal to everyone else that says: *I'm not in your triangle. I'm not like you. I'm just me.*

Me.

Non-artistic.

Me.

Scared of dogs.

Me.

Kind of triangle-obsessed.

A drop of hummus falls off my carrot and onto my shirt. I glare at the hummus. I glare at the picture of a giant baseball on the shirt. Why do all these T-shirts think they know who I am?

I scoop up the drop of hummus with a carrot, then take off the shirt and put it in the laundry. I start digging into my bureau drawer for something else, but it's mostly full of shirts my mom bought me because they're "funny and cool," and I am most definitely not that. Don't I have something that isn't baseball-related or covered in animals wearing sunglasses?

And then I remember . . .

I open my closet and rummage around, and finally I see it there in the back. The white button-down shirt I wore to that *Reaching for the Moon* bookstore event. Katherine Johnson wasn't there, but there was a lady from NASA who talked about Katherine's work. I sat in a packed audience surrounded by people like me who were interested in the same thing. Now, that was cool!

I take out the shirt and look at it closely. There's a little embroidered emblem of a bird on the top right. It's a puffin. Like the bird on the cereal box that my mom gets. And its beak has some fabulous triangle action going on. Katherine Johnson would approve.

I pull on the shirt and button it up. I guess I've grown, because it's super snug. But it feels good, like I'm still surrounded by all those people at the bookstore. I tuck the shirt into my sweatpants. If Clark Kent merged his button-down outfit with his spandex one, I bet he'd end up with something like this.

Plus, I remember reading on the back of the cereal box that puffins can fly at fifty-five miles an hour. That'd be great for getting away from people like Cal Carpenter.

I look in the mirror. The shirt clearly sends the message *Don't expect me to be like anyone else.*

It's perfect.

T

MONDAY, APRIL 30

Wet concrete.
Sirens.
Shadows.
Never safe to sleep.

But so
very
tired.

Peko snuggles up.
Her fur warm against me.
Follow her breath.
Breathe with her.

Trust
her.
Only
her.

One breath at a time.
Still here.

JACK

TUESDAY, MAY 1

ON TUESDAY, I get up super early and head to the kitchen to make myself a couple peanut-butter-and-jelly sandwiches. It's still mostly dark out, but today's the first day of turkey season, and Uncle Sid's picking me up soon to go hunting before school.

My dad would be joining us if he were here, but these days he spends most of the week up in northern Vermont on a construction job.

Based on the cold mug of tea sitting on the counter, my mom's up too. She's probably outside. I pull on my coat and take my sandwiches out the door. I find her around back. She's been at her garden beds for weeks now, but mostly she's only been able to look at them. "Scheming," she said. But I guess it's finally the day to start loosening up the dirt, because she's dragging her shovels and everything out of the shed. Her shift at the hospital doesn't start until two in the afternoon on Tuesdays.

"You gonna stick around and help me?" she calls when she sees me.

I shake my head, and just as I'm telling her that Uncle Sid will be here any minute, we hear his pickup truck coming up the driveway. I hustle back to meet him, taking the long way around, because I never go on the east side of the barn. Not since the day Alex died.

Uncle Sid is out of the truck, leaning against it like he's been waiting for hours. I bet he thinks I'm still in bed and he's going to shame me when I come out of the house all groggy. Too bad I'm not. And too bad I'm a good shot with a pine cone.

"Hey!" he calls, rubbing the side of his arm where I beaned him. "Watch it, or you'll be running after those turkeys, trying to catch them with your bare hands."

I pick up my gun from where I left it on the porch. "Remember? I'm packing my own firepower this year."

"You're lucky you passed your hunting license test."

"As if I needed luck. I knew every single answer."

"Only because you've got the best teacher." He puts his arm around my shoulder. "I'd say *that's* pretty lucky." He laughs and releases me. "Okay, hop in. Let's go get those turkeys."

Uncle Sid turns up the radio, and soon we're bumping

35

down our dirt driveway. "So how's school?" he asks, pulling onto the main road.

"It's good, but yesterday was annoying. This lady from the state showed up to check out our school. She acted like she knew way more than us. Like we were hicks or something."

"We get the short end of the stick up here in the hills." Uncle Sid shakes his head. "The government likes to poke its nose in our business because they don't trust folks like us. Not even with our schools." The radio goes to static, like it always does when we dip below the hillside, and Uncle Sid flips it off. "Those people don't even get hunting. Don't even get that eating turkey from the grocery store is way worse. Especially for the turkey."

He parks the truck on the side of the road near our hunting spot and cuts the engine. "Just remember, when it comes to your life, your school, your town, you name it . . ." He pokes a finger at my chest. "You know best."

I'm happy that Uncle Sid gets it—and his words make me feel better. So does hunting. It's peaceful in the woods and just the way I like it. A test of our stealth as we try to slip noiselessly down the trails in the fog of the morning. Uncle Sid and I have gotten so good at communicating with tiny movements that it's like we have our own language.

Once we get to our spot with a good sight line, I get down low with my back to a tree and wait. By now, I'm used to staying as still as possible, but it used to take all the effort I had. I remember my first hunting trip with Uncle Sid, when I was nine and he caught a buck. I was proud to have helped, but when we got home, it was clear that Alex was upset over the whole hunting thing. The night we were going to eat the venison, Alex didn't want to come to the table. But my dad forced him to sit with us, saying, "No son of mine is going to be a vegetarian!" So Alex stayed at the table, and even though he was only five at the time, he didn't even cry, because he'd already learned not to in front of our dad.

Alex missed a lot of dinners after that. He'd have stomachaches, and my mom would bring toast and milk up to his room, where he'd make tons of animal drawings. Sometimes he'd cut them out and make little houses for them. A book would become a tent. His laundry basket would turn into a lake for the ducks. Who were definitely not being shot down by hunters.

Uncle Sid has been making a hen call with his slate, and after a long wait we hear a rustling in the bushes. Quickly, Uncle Sid gets his shotgun in position and trains it in the direction of the sound. He's waiting for it to come into view, until he sees its beard.

He looks at me. He's telling me to get my gun ready.

I've been waiting for this. The moment when I'm the one who gets to take the shot. I lift up my gun, train it, and wait, trying to keep my hand as steady as possible.

But when the turkey and its beard come into view, I don't pull the trigger.

Because all I can think about is Alex.

I can tell Uncle Sid is eyeing me, but he doesn't give me a hard time about it. Instead, he pulls his trigger and takes the bird down.

"You'll get it next time," he says, patting me on the back as we go to get the turkey.

I look at the bird. One shot. No suffering.

If it was going to end up as someone's dinner anyway, at least it got to live a life with no cages, right?

LIBBY

TUESDAY, MAY 1

I'M RIGHT IN the middle of a dream involving huge paint cans when the lights go on in my room. I open one eye to see Rex going through his shirt drawer.

I cover my face with my pillow. "What time is it?"

Rex ignores me.

I roll over to see the clock next to my bed: 5:45. "Really?" I say. "You gotta wake me up at five forty-five in the morning?"

"If I have to be up, so should you." He takes out a short-sleeve polo shirt with the L&H Wholesalers insignia and changes into it. "No one respects lazy." He crosses the room to flick me on the forehead before heading out.

That's when my mom shows up in the doorway. "Rex! I didn't hear you come in. Getting ready for your shift too?"

She doesn't even try to be quiet, because obviously anyone worth anything is already awake.

"Wally! Rex is here!" she shouts.

"Thanks for washing my shirts," Rex says.

"Hey, buddy. How's it going?" My dad's fresh out of the shower, and his volume is set to extra-loud. He and Rex do their special high-five/fist-bump combo right in the doorway of my room. I roll over to face the wall.

"Want to come over for dinner tomorrow night?" my mom asks. "I'm trying out a new chicken recipe."

"Aren't Wednesday nights softball games?"

My dad laughs. "You haven't heard? Libby quit the team."

Honestly.

"Are you kidding?" Rex raises his voice. "Really, Libs. After all I did to make you the catcher that you are?"

I glare at the wall. So maybe he did teach me to catch way back when he was occasionally a nice brother, but that shouldn't require payment of a lifetime of servitude.

I roll back over so I can stick my tongue out at him.

"And get this," my dad tells Rex. "Yesterday she got so carried away with some stupid art project that I had to go over to that school to bail her out."

"It wasn't stupid," I say. "And you didn't bail me—"

"You think you should be talking back right now?" my mom snaps.

"You need to quit babying her and letting her live in her pretend world," Rex says. "She should pull her weight around the house more."

I glare at him. "Ha! You have your own apartment. You shouldn't even be here."

He cocks his head. Then he takes a sock from his pile of dirty laundry and flings it at me. "I can be anywhere I want to be."

࿐

When they've all finally left the house, I throw Rex's sock against the wall. It makes the least satisfying noise ever.

What does he know? So what if I sometimes want to live in a pretend world? It's better than this one.

I take the card out from under my pillow to remind me. *You are amazing.*

Those three words. They're the reason I get out of bed.

I pull on an orange shirt, a yellow polka-dot sweatshirt, and red pants. I can be my own sunrise. Because I *am* amazing.

࿐

It's a long walk to school, but it's better than hanging around at the bus stop now that Adrianna's not talking to me. She's not exactly subtle about it either.

An empty chips bag skipping along the sidewalk on a gust of wind is the only company I need.

I like that my route takes me through downtown. It's quiet, and the shops are still closed. I stop in front of the art supply shop. In the display window are giant flowers made out of tissue paper, along with the words SPRING IS HERE! PLANT YOUR SEEDS! PUT BEAUTY INTO THE WORLD! I press my nose against the glass. It's like the flowers are leaping out of the earth. Like they just needed someone to plant that seed and then they shot themselves up through the dirt and into the air like a rocket.

I study the buds on a bush next to a nearby bench. All around town, bushes just like this, with those yellow flowers, are blooming. But this one is still sealed up tight.

Maybe things would be easier if I could do a better job of staying closed-up. Like if I didn't wear my yellow polka-dot sweatshirt all the time. Maybe then Danielle wouldn't have teased me, and I wouldn't have lost my temper and punched her, and I'd still be on the softball team.

I look back at the art supply store. Those flowers in the window sure are glorious.

VINCENT

TUESDAY, MAY 1

THE NEXT MORNING, I put on my this-is-who-I-am puffin shirt and tuck it into my sweatpants. Mom's at the kitchen table on her computer when I come downstairs. She's friends with lots of other art shop owners, and they're always sharing pictures of their new window displays. She looks up and automatically holds her arms out for a hug, but as soon as she sees me, her eyes widen. "That's not what you're wearing to school, is it?"

I imagine myself as Clark Kent and try to stand tall. "It is."

"Is something special going on today?"

"Not really."

She presses her lips together. "The shirt's super small on you."

"I like it small. And I really like puffins. Actually, do we have any of that Puffins cereal?"

My mom is still eyeing me suspiciously. "I don't know. Check in the cupboard."

I dig way into the back—suddenly there's nothing I want more in the world than this cereal.

"Here it is!" I hold it up like a trophy.

I can feel my mom's eyes on me as I pour the cereal and hide behind the box. "Did you know that puffins spend eight months alone in the northern oceans, which is one of the harshest environments on the planet?"

"I did not know that, Vincent."

"Well, it's true."

I don't have to glance at her to know that she's still looking at me.

"Are they one of those flightless birds?" she says.

"Not at all. Puffins can flap their wings very fast. Four hundred times a minute is what is says here."

"And they actually fly when they do that? Because a chicken can flap its—"

"They're nothing like a chicken, Mom. Nothing."

That keeps my mom quiet for a while, and I focus on how delicious this Puffins cereal is. Crispy. Even in the milk. Quite a high-class cereal.

Quite a high-class bird.

I'm tilting the bowl to get the last of the milk when my mom says, "Vincent." I turn to look at her. "Eight months *is* a long time to be in a harsh environment. Is—"

"I know it is, Mom," I say. And then I put my bowl in the dishwasher and grab my backpack, and I'm out the door.

〜

I hear them snickering when I'm at my locker. "What kind of weirdo boy are you?" Zachary Wilkins asks.

I turn to see Cal Carpenter jab him in the arm. "You kidding? He's no boy." He slams my locker shut before I've even gotten my books and looks me in the eye. "Girl."

If a puffin can flap its wings four hundred times in a minute, that's like sixty-five times in ten seconds. That puffin would be already out of here.

"Girl." Cal Carpenter repeats it when we're all bunched up at the back of science class getting our bowls of dry beans for the foraging lab.

I can't figure out why he's calling me this. Are girls bad? Considering how much time he and his friends spend at the popular girls' lunch table, I don't think they're against them.

And I'm not actually a girl.

"Girl."

I hear it again while I'm trying to forage for the beans with a fork like any good bean-eating creature would. This time, it's Zachary Wilkins who says it. Do girls wear button-down shirts with puffins on them? Maybe he's thinking about the puffins. Maybe he knows how the male puffins help take care of the baby puffins. Also, the babies are called pufflings. Who wouldn't want to take care of a puffling?

"Girl."

I can't tell who says it this time because they pretend-cough it while we're handing in our vocab quizzes in English. Do they mean that I'm gay? How would that person behind me know whether I liked boys instead of girls? I mean, I don't particularly like either at the moment.

But Cal and his friends certainly seem confident. Would they know more about this than me?

"Girl."

In the lunch line.

I tuck my shirt in even tighter. The definition for the vocab word *surmise* pops into my head. "Infer from incomplete evidence."

And what precisely is their evidence? I don't see any single girl in the cafeteria wearing sweatpants and a button-down shirt.

"Girl."

In the hall on the way to social studies. Did Cal Carpenter call a meeting and tell everyone there was only one word they could use today? Though I do remember Zachary answering a question in science. He didn't say "girl" then. He said "paramecium."

"Girl."

When we're getting our supplies in art class.

We're supposed to be painting landscapes to practice

with vanishing points, but I just put a little bit of green at the bottom for the land and make the rest of the paper sky. Blue, blue, and more blue.

I want to draw a puffin smack in the middle of that sky, with its wings flapping so fast that it's a blur.

But I'm not artistic. And when I try, it looks like a black UFO—specifically, a UFO drawn by a three-year-old. When I try to fix it, it only makes it worse. I crumple up my paper and throw it out before anyone can see.

When I finally get home, I crawl into bed and curl into the fetal position as tears start to fall.

One point in space. Why does it have to be so hard to be one lonely point in space?

JACK

TUESDAY, MAY 1

DURING LUNCHTIME AT school, I help the youngers open their containers and clean up any spills. I've been helping out since I was ten. It was the fall after Alex died, when he should have been in first grade, that Mrs. Lincoln first asked if I'd start reading to them once a week. Today, though, is a record for spills. Two milks, one juice, and one container of crackers that immediately gets stepped on. And Joey, who's usually the messiest one, isn't even here for lunch today because he got picked up early.

I'm about to push open the door to the office to get a new roll of paper towels when I hear Mr. Sasko and Mrs. Lincoln talking inside.

"That grant is a third of our budget," Mr. Sasko is saying. "If we don't get it for next year, I don't know how we'll be able to stay open."

I freeze and pretend to examine the sponge-print butterflies Mrs. Lincoln hung up this morning.

The school might have to close?

It can't. Next year is my eighth-grade year. How could I spend it somewhere else? And what would happen to all of us? Just farmed out to a bunch of different schools in the valley, where all the students think they're better than hicks like us?

Mrs. Lincoln bursts out of the office, her eyes wide. "Oh, Jack," she says, nearly slamming into me. "I didn't realize you were there. Are you okay? Can I help you?"

I stumble over my words. "I just needed more paper towels, and I stopped . . . to look at the sponge-print butterflies."

"Oh, of course," she says. She forces a smile. "They turned out nice this year, didn't they?"

I nod. Every year, Mrs. Lincoln makes them with the youngest kids, and I remember how much Alex loved creating them. He fit so many sponge prints on the paper there was hardly room for Mrs. Lincoln's blue border. I'd never seen him that excited for a project. All of his drawings were of butterflies after that.

My whole life has been at this school. Alex loved this school. Joey needs this school.

Mrs. Lincoln grabs the extra roll of paper towels from inside the office. "Don't worry about the spill. I'll take it from here." As she walks away, she mutters, "At least that's something I can do something about."

She squats down to clean up the milk near the flag at the front of the room, and I think about how we gather around that flag every morning. But when we are saying the Pledge of Allegiance, we're not pledging to do whatever the state wants. We're pledging to uphold the Founding Fathers' ideas about freedom and independence. *With liberty and justice for all.*

For *all*. We say it every day. And I'm going to find a way to stop that lady from the state from taking our funding. I'll do whatever it takes to save our school.

LIBBY
TUESDAY, MAY 1

MY DAY AT school is as joyous as you'd expect. There's the part when I'm forced to paint over my beautiful almost-complete sunrise. And the part where kids walk past the door of the in-school suspension room, peering in, acting so pleased, like they personally predicted this would happen. It's like how everyone crowded around the gorilla enclosure on our zoo field trip when the gorilla was throwing poop at things. No one was going to turn away, but no one would ever think about being friends with that gorilla.

In-school suspension would be way more fun if I could throw poop at things.

At the end of the day, I join the funnel of kids leaving the building and get stuck behind Danielle Fisher. "Did you see Libby in the ISS room again today?" she is telling Adrianna. "Thank goodness you're not friends with her anymore. My mom says that it's best to stay away from that *whole* family. I told you what her dad was like in the office yesterday, right?"

I keep my head down, but that doesn't stop me from hearing what she says next.

"She's a bully. Just like her dad."

I make a break for it as soon as I can. No way can I get on that bus. I'll go directly home, like my dad said—I'll just do it the walking way. I try my best to breathe.

Walking through town is a lot different in the afternoon, with all the businesses open. There are people all over the place, strolling on the sidewalks, and it's finally warm enough for a few to be sitting at the tables outside the bagel place. Near Happy Dental, there's a little boy with a buzz cut clinging to a bench and screaming. Tears are running down his face.

"Stop making a scene," his mom growls. "Let's go."

Maybe I'm the person watching the gorilla throw poop around now, but I can't help myself. Plus, the little boy's face is so desperate. Like letting go of the bench would mean certain death.

"I won't go," he cries.

"Joseph Sebastian Kelligan, you let go this instant," his mom orders.

"But I'm scared," he wails.

"We came all this way . . ." His mom starts to pry his fingers off the bench. "Don't be such a crybaby."

The boy looks up at her, his eyes wide, and I know exactly why: Now even she can't be trusted.

I watch as she carries him, screaming, into the dentist's office, and I sink down onto the bench, running my hand along the part where his little fingers were clinging.

I wish I could run inside and tell him that I know what it feels like to look up into the eyes of the person who is supposed to love you most and wonder if they do. I pull out my index card that tells me that I'm amazing. I let out a long breath as I look at it. He needs it more than I do.

I fish one of the colored pencils from my bag and write in little letters along the ridge of the mountain, *And you are not alone!* I look around for where to leave it. The bush next to the bench is the one with the closed-up buds from this morning. But not all the buds are closed up now! One glorious purple flower has burst forth!

I set the index card in the bush, next to the flower, right where he'll see it when he comes out, and skip the rest of the way home. Even though I don't have the amazing index card in my backpack, somehow I'm a whole lot lighter on my feet.

TUESDAY, MAY 1

An empty stomach can feel like freedom.
Nothing weighing you down.
Zero.
Zip.
Who needs to eat?

But then it's over and it's back to being
a gaping black hole,
sucking all thoughts from the brain
except for food.

And Peko.
I always save some of my thoughts for her.

JACK
WEDNESDAY, MAY 2

MY DAD'S COMING home from his job tonight, and we're celebrating by eating the turkey Uncle Sid bagged. My mom's been brining it for a day. She even roasted the last sweet potatoes from the root cellar.

As soon as we hear my dad's truck in the driveway, my mom and I burst onto the porch. My dad doesn't say anything when he gets to us. He just pulls each of us into a long hug. He smells like asphalt and coffee, and it feels good to have the solid wall of his body back in our house. The money he makes doing construction is good, but two weeks is a long time to be away from home.

Uncle Sid arrives, and it's a real celebration. He's come straight here from his work, not wanting to miss a second with his older brother.

Once we're all sitting down with heaping plates, Dad

tucks into his turkey. "I saw our old neighbors Bobby and Phil the other night," he announces.

"Yeah?" Uncle Sid says. "How they doing?"

"Real good. They've been working to keep our Second Amendment safe. Been circulating a petition in the towns around them up north." My dad reaches for the salt. "I went to a community dinner with them, and they must have collected a hundred signatures in an hour. Those two don't mess around."

Uncle Sid starts talking about the time they took him out on their snowmobiles in the middle of a snowstorm, but I stop listening because that's when it hits me—what if we did a petition to keep the school open?

I eye my dad, laughing with Uncle Sid. Will he think it's a good idea? Will he think I can pull it off?

When my dad pushes his plate away, he thumps me on the back. "That was one tasty turkey. So, tell me, Jack, how's it going? You've been beating those other kids at football?"

"Yeah, we've been playing."

"And have you been winning?"

"Yeah, but . . ."

"But what?" he says.

I look between my dad and my mom. "But things at school aren't great. The state is threatening to take away our grant money."

My dad crosses his arms. "On what grounds?"

"I'm not sure, but this lady from the state came to see us, acting like we just crawled out from under a rock."

My mom puts down the serving spoon. "But our school needs that money to stay open."

I nod. "That's what Mr. Sasko said too."

She shakes her head. "Anyone who thinks it's a good idea to bus little kids down that hill in winter has lost their mind. It's not safe!"

I swallow and try to sit up as straight as my dad. "No, but I think I have a plan."

"A plan?" my dad says.

I nod and try to keep my voice level. "What if I started a petition like your friends up north? What if I got signatures from everyone in Haycock?"

My dad stops eating, his fork poised in the air. "You think that would convince the state?"

I can't tell if it's a real question, or if he thinks it's a ridiculous idea to start with.

I look him in the eye, just like he's taught me. "I think it's worth a try. They shouldn't get to boss us around."

"But actually, it's not just the state you'd need to convince. It's the new consolidated school board," Uncle Sid says. "You remember how we got merged with the big school district down in the valley, right? That new board might claim they're looking out for our interests, but they'd steamroll this whole mountain if it meant more parking down there."

"I'd bet they'd be happy to have a reason to close our school and get more kids for their schools," my dad adds. "More kids mean more money."

"Still, we can play to their best intentions," my mom says. "They're always saying that they want to hear from 'all voices,' so let's see what happens when they do."

Uncle Sid smiles at me. "So you're gonna call their bluff and go to the next school board meeting, armed with a petition full of signatures from everyone in Haycock? They won't have the nerve to turn you away!"

My dad pushes up from his chair and walks over to the window. "Why won't they let us be? This is David versus Goliath."

"But, Dad," I say, standing up too, "doesn't David beat Goliath in the end?"

He looks at me, and I don't look away. "I promise to take down Goliath," I say.

And even though I don't say it out loud, what I'm thinking is: *I promise to make you proud.*

VINCENT
WEDNESDAY, MAY 2

"HOW ARE YOU feeling this morning?"

My mom's at my bedroom door.

Or at least I assume she is. I haven't opened my eyes yet.

"Fine," I mumble.

"Are you going to get dressed?"

Ha. Great question. Maybe I'll go to school naked.

"Vincent?"

"Yes, Mom, I am going to get dressed." I open my eyes and push up to my elbows just to prove my point. She's got to get to work soon anyway. This coming weekend is the store's big anniversary sale.

"Make good choices today, okay?" she says. She pauses and then crosses the room to give me a hug. "I love you," she says into my hair. Her new face cream smells like oranges. When she releases me, she holds me by the shoulders. "I don't want to see you hurt."

"I know," I say. "Thanks."

Then she leaves, and I'm left staring at the button-down shirt hanging over my chair. I eye the motorcycling-sloth shirt still on the floor. No way can I wear that.

I guess I just don't get middle school. In elementary school, no one cared what shirt I wore. Except that they never actually talked to me, so how would I know.

How am I supposed to make good choices? Have I ever made good choices?

I decide to skip the decision for now, and when I hear my mom in the shower, I put on my bathrobe and head to the kitchen. I pour myself a bowl of my trusty Puffins cereal. Those birds would never make fun of me. They would get me. I bet they know what it's like to be bullied—I mean, the box says their nickname is "the clowns of the sea."

I stare at the cereal box as I eat and read more. It says that while puffins are out there on the ocean for all those months, they'll float on the surface of the water and just go up and down with the waves. Up and down. Up and down. Totally chill.

I need to be like that.

It also says that they use their wings to basically fly through the water. And, really, who cares if you're called "the clown of the sea" if you can do that?

I hear Mom's shower shut off, and I try to look as chill

as chill can be when she comes out of the bathroom, rub-bing gel into her short, spiky hair.

"Are you all right with me leaving early, Vincent? Miranda called and was having a crisis—"

"Yeah, it's fine."

She kisses the top of my head again. "You sure?" She starts to sift through her purse for her lipstick. She chooses the bright-purple one today.

"Yeah. I got this," I say.

I watch my mom apply her lipstick and then pull on the embroidered denim jacket that her friend June sent her. My mom can wear what she wants because she's found her people.

But I'm not my mom.

I'm a point in space. Out in the ocean. With no people.

I look at the photo on the box of the puffin flying. I trace the triangle of its beak. At least I have triangles to keep me company. I trace the triangle you get when you divide the rectangular box in two. I trace the triangle made by my spoon resting on the side of my bowl. One triangle at a time, I will get through this.

As soon as my mom is out the door, I wash out my bowl and slip back into my bedroom.

I look at my Katherine Johnson poster. Then I look at the shirt. There are two triangles at the tip of the collar. One on the left. One on the right. I take a deep breath.

I put on a clean undershirt, and then I put that button-down right over it.

Because if I wear something different, the bullies win. And they don't get to win.

The puffins and I get to win.

I walk to school over the waves of the Seattle hills. Up and down. Through the fog. Through the rain. Riding wave after wave.

Just like a good puffin.

WEDNESDAY, MAY 2

Now I get to wear
eyeliner
if I want.

No one looks at me.
No one cares
now.

LIBBY

WEDNESDAY, MAY 2

MY DAD DIDN'T care that I didn't take the bus home yesterday, but my mom did—and she confronted me when I got home. "I haven't worked hard all my life just for you to be one of those low-class kids loitering around, getting into trouble," she reminded me while dipping the egg-yolky chicken into bread crumbs. I told her that I had walked straight home (the bench outside the dentist's office was directly on my way) and that it's healthy to breathe fresh air once in a while. But she made me feel like one of those shoplifting kids at the 7-Eleven when she turned her beady eyes on me.

So when the dismissal bell rings on Wednesday, I tuck my head down and climb the stairs of the bus. My mom will be at work when I get home, but she's made sure that my dad will be watching for me.

I'm feeling pretty gross when I get dropped off—the

whole ride I had to listen to Adrianna and Danielle talk extra-loud about how everyone would be going to Danielle's house for pizza on Friday after practice. So I don't even mind when my dad greets me with one of his bad jokes—at least it's better than getting yelled at.

"Libby," my dad says, "what do you call a can of soup that eats other cans of soup?"

I pause in the driveway. "I don't know. What?"

He checks the oil of the engine he's working on. "A *can*nibal."

"Good one," I say.

"You could have at least tried to guess," he yells as I head inside.

So much for not getting yelled at—I should have figured. My dad likes to think he's the joking kind of dad, even though he doesn't actually smile when he tells jokes. It's more like he's testing me. Like the drill sergeant of jokes.

The phone rings as soon as I walk in the kitchen. It's my mom at work.

"How was your day?" she says.

"Fine," I say. At least today wasn't in-school suspension.

"Good," she says. I can tell she's sucking on a cough drop. She's been getting over a cold for weeks. "So, your dad and I were thinking. When Rex was your age, he was already making money."

Selling fake Pokémon cards at school. What a role model.

"But we're fair. We're not going to insist that you do that." She sucks hard on her cough drop. I can practically smell the menthol from here. "Instead, we think Rex is right. It's time for you to start helping around the house more."

More? I already take out the trash, put away the dishes, and do my own laundry. "Doing what?"

"Doing the dinner prep. If you're not going to have softball after school anymore, you've got to find something useful to do with that time."

"I am doing—"

"Don't try to tell me that you playing with crayons is somehow helping the family."

"They're colored pencils," I mumble.

"What was that?"

"What about homework?" I say.

"You have plenty of time to do that before you go to bed. Now, with you doing the chopping and prepping before I get home, it'll be just like on the cooking shows when they can have a dinner ready in minutes. I even printed out tonight's recipe for you. Do you see it on top of the microwave?"

There it is. Chicken ratatouille. "Yeah, I see it."

"Good. We'll end up with healthy dinners, and you'll learn the value of hard work."

I finger the recipe. So many things that need to be chopped.

"Real, practical work," she's saying. "Not just some silly worksheets at school. And definitely not coloring . . ."

Don't argue, I tell myself. *It will only make things worse.*

I look down and realize I've just crumpled the recipe into a ball.

"Right, Mom." I flatten out the recipe against the edge of the counter.

"And when you're done chopping up each ingredient, put them each in their own Ziploc bag because they're going into the pan at different times."

"But that's so many plastic baggies. That's not good for the environme—"

"And I don't have time to do dishes for an extra hour tonight. Don't give me lip. It's the closest we have to the little glass bowls they use on the cooking shows."

I close my eyes. "I'll have it ready when you get home."

"Good for you," she says. "I'll be there as soon as I can, and Rex is coming tonight, too, so put the tablecloth on." And then she hangs up.

Rex is coming—isn't that nice! I start pulling ingredients out of the fridge and slamming them onto the counter. Green peppers. Eggplant. Zucchini. I miss the counter when I pull out the tomato, and it falls to the floor with a splat.

I sit down next to the tomato. It's oozing juice into a gap in the linoleum.

My parents get me new shoes when I need them, right?

My mom didn't have that growing up, and she reminds me every time I get a new pair that I should be grateful.

I glare at the tomato, but I pick it up and put it on the counter before it can make any more of a mess. I don't like tomatoes. I don't even like chicken.

At least the eggplant looks like it has a face. I turn it so it can glare at the tomato too.

I examine the green pepper and then turn it on its side so its stem is like a long, curly nose, and it's *also* glaring at the tomato.

Maybe I shouldn't be making vegetables glare at each other. Maybe I'm just as bad as the rest of my family. But I don't want to be. I want to make things better for people, not worse.

The problem is, most people aren't exactly easy to like.

It's only when I hear my dad coming inside to use the bathroom that I remember I'm supposed to be chopping the vegetables.

I'm putting the final ingredient into its own special baggie when my mom gets home at 6:10.

"Finally, you've done something useful," she says when she sees everything chopped and bagged. "That's my girl." She turns on the stove and launches into a whirlwind of activity.

Chopping zucchini into ridiculously small pieces and then sealing them into plastic that will end up in a landfill: It's all I'm good for.

"Do you know what Dan—"

"Sorry," she says. "I need to focus right now."

I watch her, waiting to tell her about how rude Danielle and Adrianna are being, but before I get the chance, Rex walks in.

He drops his sweatshirt on one chair and sinks into another. "I'm tired."

My mom turns to look at him. "How was your day?" she says.

Rex gives a big sigh. "They had me in the freezer section, showing the new guy how to operate the pallet jack."

"Look at you. Pulling in a paycheck. Training others." My mom beams at Rex. "I'm so proud of you. To think I used to worry you were gonna turn out like your uncle."

"I'd like to see Uncle Wade make it through one whole shift in the freezer," Rex says. "The gloves they give you don't do squat and . . ."

My mom continues to look at Rex like he's the best thing that's ever happened. When does she ever pause her cooking long enough to look at me? I decide to read the label on the can of tomatoes. Then I move on to the cereal boxes on the counter. You can learn a lot from those boxes of wholesome cereal.

"Could you move, Libby?" my mom says. "I need to get to the flour."

I look up at her, but she's focused on the flour behind me.

"Come on, Libs," Rex says. "Get with the program."

69

I roll my eyes but leave the room. No matter what I do, I'm always in the way.

After dinner, I head to my room, close my door, and take out my colored pencils and glitter glue. I took a stack of extra index cards from Mr. Cruck's pile while he went on and on about the importance of a good concluding sentence. He did say they were there in case we needed more, so I've got no guilt about that.

I start filling the index cards with drawings. One gets heart-shaped flowers growing out of the ground, and the words *I'm rooting for you* written across the dirt. Another gets a frog leaping across heart-shaped lily pads that say *Jump for joy! You're terrific!* and I use the glitter glue to trace the arcs of his hops. I fill one whole index card with sunset colors and make the silhouette of a bird flying across it. I don't know what to write, though. I hold it up to study it. The bird looks lonely. Too lonely. I add another bird flying behind it. Then I add another and another until there's a whole V of birds flying behind it. I write: *Fly free! We're right behind you.*

Every time I think about my family, I do another index card.

The way my dad reamed out the pizza delivery guy last week because it took him an extra ten minutes to get to our house—even though there was an accident downtown that had blocked everything up—and then he refused to pay.

The way at dinner my mom loudly observed how much weight a woman at the other end of our street has gained.

The way Rex needles me every chance he gets.

Each one gets an index card.

My parents come to wish me a good night around nine thirty, and I quickly cover the index cards with a blanket.

"We like what we saw today," my mom says.

"Showing respect," my dad says. "Like you should be."

I shift the blanket a few inches to cover a card that's sticking out.

"I think this grounding is going to teach you more than you expect," my mom says.

"She's lucky she's got us as parents," my dad says, putting his arm around my mom. "Because when you're the daughter of Wally Delmar, you start ten steps ahead of everyone else."

When they finally disappear to watch TV in the living room, I look around at Rex's clothes all over the place. I look at the pockmarks in the ceiling from his baseball.

I lift the blanket and look at my index cards.

They are so different from anything my parents or brother would ever think to make. And they *are* useful.

Something that can make someone's day better.

I picture that boy on the bench outside the dentist's office. I hope he was able to find the one I left for him.

I take a deep breath. These index cards can't stay here. They belong out in the world.

Yes.

I gather them up and silently slip out of my window like a secret agent. Like the most useful, hardworking secret agent there is.

Who happens to be wielding a fistful of paper love bombs.

Once I'm in town, I look around. There are a few people heading to the late movie, but the sidewalks are mostly empty.

I start to stick the index cards all over the place—in a window box outside the pharmacy; in the bike rack at the library; attached to an ATM; in the window of the art supply store; on the steps into the ice cream shops; on a bulletin board outside the senior center; and stuck into the hedge between the hardware store and the post office. Even if no one thinks to pick one up, at least they're adding more flowers and sunshine to the world. That has to count for something.

Finally, I reach the bush near the dentist's office, and the card I left there is gone! Did someone find it? Did they read it? Did the dandelion and mountain and sunrise make them smile? Could I actually have made someone I don't even know smile?

I put another card in its place. That kid can't be the only one who doesn't like going to the dentist.

I still have two cards left when I look at the time and realize my mom's show is ending soon. I need to get back home.

When I get close, I relax. My room is still dark. There's no silhouette of my mom in my window, waiting to pounce.

But then I hear my dad talking . . . outside! He's in the driveway, pacing and talking on his phone, trying to get some customer to pay up. "I'm not going to tell you again I don't do this work for free," he says.

When his back is to me, I cross the driveway and press myself against the side of the house.

"I know how much you thought it was going to cost," he says, "but it's not my fault the parts had to be special-ordered. That comes at a premium price."

The motion-sensor lamp on the garage is lighting up our driveway, but I'm safe in the shadows. I just have to not make any noise.

Through the window, I can see my mom stand up from her chair and cross the living room. I know a new show is coming on now, but it's that one she's always complaining about, with the announcer who winks too much. Could she be going to check on me?

I don't have much time.

When my dad turns back toward the garage, I go for it. I heft myself up and through the window as quick as I can.

I exhale and crawl into bed. I've barely pulled up the covers when I hear my mom come into the hallway. I quickly curl onto my side, facing the wall, and a moment later my door creaks as she peeks in.

I picture the index card I left at the art supply store.

The one with a flower trying to reach the sunshine that said *I'm rooting for you.*

My parents might see themselves as strong and sturdy, like concrete.

Too bad I'm that dandelion sprouting through the cracks.

JACK
THURSDAY, MAY 3

ON THURSDAY MORNING, I get to school early. I'm planning to tell Mr. Sasko my idea for a petition. But before I can even get inside, one of the girls on the playground needs help tying her shoes and two other kids ask me to settle who gets the next turn on the swing. Before I know it, the playground is filling up and Joey is at my shirt, tugging for a lift to the basketball hoop.

I kneel down so I'm eye to eye with Joey. "You and me, we've got a mission today. Different from basketball," I whisper. "But just as important. Even more important."

Joey's eyes go wide. "What?"

"You know how if we have a problem, then Mr. Sasko and Mrs. Lincoln will help us out?" I say. "Well, now they have a problem. And we're going to help them. You in?"

Joey can't nod fast enough.

"You and I will go into the building early, and I'll go into the office to talk to them. Can you make sure all of Mrs. Lincoln's teaching supplies are ready for her?"

His eyes get wider. "Like her whiteboard markers?"

"And the lined paper she uses for the morning warm-up."

"And the pencils and extra erasers!" he adds. "I'll get it all ready!"

Joey and I slip into the building, and he goes right to the whiteboard and starts lining everything up.

Mr. Sasko and Mrs. Lincoln are in the office when I knock, and both look surprised when I blurt out, "I'd like to help."

"You're always such a help around here," Mrs. Lincoln says. "I don't know what we'd do without you."

"Thanks," I say. "But this is different—I heard what you said about what could happen if we don't get that grant from the state."

"Oh no, Jack," Mr. Sasko cuts in. "I'm sorry we weren't quieter. I don't want you to have to worry about this."

"That's okay, because I have a plan." I stand up straight. "I'd like to collect petition signatures from the people in this town in support of our school. We could deliver it to that new school board and send a copy to the lady from the state."

Mr. Sasko tilts his head. I swear there's a new spark in his eye.

"I always like how you think, Jack." Mr. Sasko leans

forward and looks at Mrs. Lincoln. "I'd say it's worth a shot. We could deliver it at the school board meeting next Wednesday."

"Sure." Mrs. Lincoln nods. "We can make copies of the petition here. And perhaps Jack could spend his community service time on it later this afternoon. As it is providing a service to the community."

"I most certainly agree." Mr. Sasko looks at me. "Why don't you use our writing block this morning to draft the language for the petition. Do you think you can organize the other older kids to help you collect signatures?"

"Definitely."

And suddenly a plan is in motion. Even Joey is excited about collecting signatures—so excited that I'm pretty sure he doesn't quite understand why we're doing it.

By the time school is over, I've got twenty copies of a petition and all of the older kids ready to go door-to-door to get signatures this weekend. When Sturgis tries to make an excuse about how he has to babysit his younger siblings, I tell him to bring them along.

"We're an army," I tell him. "Because this is war."

The state might think they have all the power, but they don't know who they've poked.

T

FRIDAY, MAY 4

Ketchup.
The Sunshine Drop-in Center got a donation.
Ten giant tubs of ketchup.
Ketchup on pasta.
Ketchup on beans.
Ketchup on bread that gets dropped off on its expiration
date.
Uncle Eddie always said ketchup counted as a vegetable
if you ate enough of it.
Peko drinks from her new
cleaned-out
non-ketchupy
giant tub
water dish.

The rain fills it back up.
Drip,
drip,
drip.
A reminder that
sometimes
an expiration date
is just a suggestion.
Sometimes
it's possible to keep going.
Keep
going
for longer than what
anyone else
would expect.

VINCENT
FRIDAY, MAY 4

FOR PE TODAY, I'm "playing basketball," and I am successful in that I stay away from Cal and his friends and don't get hit in the face by the ball. But that's the easy part. It's the time in the locker room that requires detailed planning to minimize exposure.

Five minutes and thirty-five seconds in the bathroom stall. Then after the bell has rung and when everyone is gone, I'll have one minute and twenty-five seconds to grab my books and get to class. At least that was the plan.

Except that when I go to get my books, Cal and his friends are still there.

"Did you seriously just put that same shirt back on?" Cal says.

"Gross, man."

I think that's Zachary talking, but I don't look up, so I'm not sure.

"How many days has it been?"

Stay focused. Just get your books. I slip past them.

"Hey! We're talking to you!"

I pick up my stack of notebooks and binders. I focus on the cover of my math notebook, where I've drawn exactly one hundred and eight overlapping triangles of various sizes.

I turn to face them. "I am wearing an undershirt underneath. And I change that every day. And I haven't spilled anything on it." Mostly because I've stopped eating lunch in the cafeteria. I can make a picnic blanket out of paper towels in the accessible bathroom in the music wing, which nobody ever uses during lunchtime.

Zachary and the others are laughing, but Cal comes toward me. "Do you respect the people at this school?"

Respect them? "Uh . . . I guess?"

"Then show respect for their eyes and change out of that shirt."

"Everything okay over there?" It's Ms. Lemmick's voice from the PE office.

"Yep. Everything's fine!" Cal says, and I slip out the door and walk away as fast as my legs can go.

I get to social studies out of breath and sink into my seat. Next time, I'll only leave one minute and seven seconds to get here. And I'll bring my books into the bathroom stall with me.

I squeeze my eyes shut while Mr. Henderson asks if there are any questions from the homework.

The thing about Clark Kent and Katherine Johnson is that they weren't just a boring, nerdy boy and a girl who could see triangles. They were people who flew! Katherine, because it was her math that calculated the trajectory of that first rocket, and Clark Kent, well, because of the cape.

But where's my cape? Where's the rocket I've calculated the trajectory for?

What if I'm just a boring, nerdy boy who sees triangles and who's always almost about to get stuffed into a locker—and nothing else.

When social studies is finally over, I pick up my books and head into the crowded hallway. At least now I get to go to math.

But that's when I hear Cal Carpenter's voice at my ear. "I told you to change out of that shirt, didn't I? Didn't I?"

Before I know what's happening, I feel my shirt being pulled out from my waistband and being tugged up, up, up. I want to fight back, but my arms are pinned in the air as the shirt gets stuck.

I can't see anything, but I can hear. My voice. Panicked. Cal's laugh and the sound of other kids in the hallway, not wanting to miss a second of this.

Then I hear Mr. Henderson.

He's coming. But not fast enough.

Cal tugs my undershirt up around my head too. Pop,

pop, pop—the buttons fly off my puffin shirt—and then both shirts are gone.

My bright-white, bony chest suddenly exposed.

I can see now, but it's not good. So many eyes watching. No one stepping in to do something.

Cal lets go of my arms. Mostly because he's laughing so hard. He tosses my shirts to a kid on the far side of the hallway, and I picture the puffin with its triangle beak and its short, sturdy black wings. Because it doesn't ride the ocean waves forever. It can fly.

It's time for this puffin to take flight.

I fly down that hallway. Away from everyone. I fly out the double doors at the back of the school, into the rain, and right past the PE field. Too bad Ms. Lemmick misses out on seeing the fastest speed I've ever gone.

I run until I can no longer breathe. Like I'm going to pass out and throw up at the same time.

Everything looks blurry, which is fine, because it means I can't see all the people wondering why a kid who should clearly be wearing a shirt isn't.

I stop in an alley and double over, convinced that I'm about to meet the chicken parmesan I had for lunch. Instead, I just retch. I can't even throw up right.

I'm still staring at my pathetic puddle of spit on the concrete when I realize there's someone in the alley with me.

"You want this?" they say, holding out a shirt.

I try to say yes, but I'm still gulping for air. Desperate to cover my chest, I pull the shirt on. It's a basketball shirt—and it's big and dirty, but better than no shirt.

By the time I'm able to form words and look up, the person is disappearing around the corner. I can just make out a green raincoat.

I speak up anyway, and my "Thank you" echoes down the alley—but the only response is the sound of a dog barking.

JACK

SATURDAY, MAY 5

I PROMISED JOEY we could collect petition signatures together today, so I meet him in front of his family's double-wide. They have a tire swing tied to a tree, and Joey is draped over the tire facedown, spinning, spinning, and spinning. He's wearing one of his hockey jerseys. The kid is a speed demon on ice, and his mom already has him in a hockey league. I went to a couple of his games this winter, and even though he was a head shorter than everyone else, he could zip by them with the puck no problem.

"You dizzy?" I ask when he sees me and stands up.

He grins and staggers to the side. "No."

I laugh and give Joey's buzz cut a rub as he staggers back past me, giggling. "Nice jersey."

He looks down at it. "My mom made me wear it."

"You don't like it?"

He glances at their trailer and whispers, "I wish it was a basketball jersey."

"But you're really good at hockey. I've seen you."

"It's not my favorite sport." He shrugs. "I don't like the hitting."

I think back to the games I saw. "The squirt division doesn't have body checking, does it?"

"No, but it's coming, and my mom's never going to let me quit. She said I was made for hockey." He kicks at the grass.

"I bet you'll be used to it by that time."

"I don't want to get used to it." He drapes himself back over the tire swing and starts spinning again. "I want to be a grown-up so I can be in charge of what sports I do. How many times do you think I'd need to spin to get to being a grown-up? A million? A gabillion?"

Before I can tell him that a gabillion isn't a real number, he blurts out, "I *love* bees. Did you know they go in circles to tell their bee friends where a good flower is? They probably go even faster than this. And did you know that lots of them are dying? My mom doesn't care, because she doesn't like getting stung by bees, but I care."

Just then, Joey's mom comes out on the stoop, and Joey switches to buzzing like a bee.

"Hi, Jack!" she calls. "Are you sure you're okay taking him?"

"Of course! We should be back around lunchtime." I

hold up my cell phone. "And we'll mostly be in areas that have reception."

I take the clipboard with the petition out of my backpack. "Want to sign?" I ask her.

She comes down onto the grass to meet me. "You bet I'm signing."

I take the clipboard back from her when she's done and call to Joey, who's still spinning. "Okay, buddy. We got our first signature—now let's go get more!"

Our first stop is the Ginters'. Mack, Deb, and Mack's brother, Hank, are all in the field, but they meet us halfway and sign the petition.

Mack watches Joey run down the row of hay, seeing how far he can leap. "Is the state gonna get rid of all the small schools and bus these little kids miles and miles?"

Hank shakes his head. "They'll try. Those politicians are all happy to talk about 'the importance of community' as long as it's their community, not ours."

I nod. "Hopefully, this will help."

Next is Mrs. Caldimore's. She's sitting on her front porch and is happy to have company. "What hoops do they want us to jump through this time?" she asks as she pours us each a big glass of milk.

"They have all kinds of random stuff they want us to do," I say. "Like fix our playground. And we're supposed to have something called a gender-neutral bathroom."

She shakes her head. "I got nothing against transgender

people, but we can't go around accommodating everyone, now, can we?" she says as she signs the petition with a pen in the shape of a flamingo.

"What are transgender people?" Joey asks as we head down the road to the next house.

"I think it's someone who feels like they're a boy when they were born a girl. Something like that."

"How about a boy who feels like he's a girl?" he asks.

"Yeah, that too," I say.

"What does it feel like to feel like a girl? Is it an inside feeling?"

"I don't know."

"I wonder," Joey continues. "You ever eaten a kiwi? Mrs. Lincoln brought us some, and they look a whole lot different on the inside than you'd think. She said it's the inside that counts, and that's true. The inside is the tastiest." He pauses. "Sometimes *people* are prickly on the outside like kiwis too."

"I guess," I say, even though I'm not sure what kiwis have to do with anything.

When we get to Nelson Palmer's house, he's out, but his new wife is there. She signs the petition while Joey makes buzzing noises to keep their baby happy.

"You're good with little kids," I tell Joey as we leave.

He looks up and gives me the sweetest smile. "So are you."

I put my arm around him. I know he's not my actual brother, but he sure feels like he could be.

Fortunately, most folks are home, and we fill up two petition sheets. We even get to my neighbor Alan Potter, who usually doesn't answer his door because he's busy watching his shows. When he hears about the bathrooms, he shakes his head. "Back in my day, we used an outhouse when we went to school. Not a fancy one either. Just one pit for everyone."

Joey's eyebrows go up. "Even in winter?"

Alan Potter tilts his head. "Yep! And it sure was cold!"

"They must have frozen their behinds off," I say to Joey, making him laugh practically the whole way back to his place.

ം℘ം

My mom isn't around when I get home, so I check my phone. She's left a voicemail telling me she's bringing eggs over to a neighbor and that our friend Ned Castleton needs to borrow our ladder. She wants me to leave it for him in the driveway.

The ladder.

She's really asking me to move the ladder?

My dad stopped using that ladder after the accident. That's when he started doing construction jobs away from home. Anything to be away from our barn and that ladder.

It had been left extended and leaning against the barn that day. I was supposed to be watching Alex but went inside for a minute to get us a snack, and when I looked out the window, I saw him going up the ladder. I dropped potato chips all over the floor and was outside in a flash, but he was all the way across the yard at the barn. And then all the way up on top of the ladder. Waving at me. A huge grin on his face.

I had never run so fast.

But I wasn't fast enough. When I was halfway there, I watched as the ladder tipped backward, like a tree crashing to earth, my little brother beneath it.

My little brother's body slammed against the ground.

I slid right next to him, heaved that ladder off his little body. It fell to the side with a clang.

Alex's body was limp, his eyes closed and his chest still rising and falling, but only slightly.

I'll never forgive those 911 people for taking so long to come.

T

SUNDAY, MAY 6

Not open on the first Sunday of the month.
What's one day without the drop-in center,
without a hot meal,
without a warm, dry place to sit for a few hours,
without a place where you belong?

What's one day
when it's been twenty-seven days on the street
after four hundred eighty-two days of
them pretending,
denying,
refusing to believe
that this is who I am?

When for me
it was like I had known it

on some level

for every single one of my

five thousand nine hundred sixty-six

days on Earth.

And once you know,

you can't not know.

It doesn't matter how much

you miss your mom's French toast.

Sometimes taking care of yourself

means leaving everything behind.

VINCENT

MONDAY, MAY 7

I OVERHEARD MY mom's whispered phone conversation with her friend June over the weekend and them talking about "tough love." Mom knew there was "an incident," because the school had called home.

"I just don't get his wearing an outgrown button-down shirt," my mom said. "Do you think it's his way of trying to make up for not having a dad? Is that what he thinks real men wear? I wish this was one of those times when you could call up your sperm donor and see if they'd be willing to give their offspring a brief talk about self-preservation."

Self-preservation.

I try to imagine some random man showing up to lecture me about self-preservation. *Don't you want to survive, son? Why are you making it so hard on yourself?*

But shouldn't self-preservation have something to do with getting to be yourself?

My mom looks all kinds of concerned when I show up in the kitchen doorway to eat breakfast on Monday morning. I'm still in my bathrobe, which I've had on all weekend.

"How are you feeling?" she asks.

Thankfully, "tough love" is not my mom's specialty.

I shrug. I pull out the new box of Puffins cereal my mom bought me—and this one has a whole new list of puffin facts on the back.

DID YOU KNOW? IN ICELAND, THE PUFFINS AREN'T BREEDING AS WELL AS THEY USED TO, BECAUSE OF THE WARMING OCEAN TEMPERATURES.

I read about how climate change has caused these fish called sand lances to swim somewhere else. And how they're the only kind of fish that the pufflings can eat.

What's going to happen to all those pufflings? Are they just going to starve to death? What if the puffins stop coming back together during breeding season? What if the environment has made it so that's impossible?

What if, no matter how hard you try, you can't survive?

I stop eating my cereal.

"Feeling any better about going back to school?" my mom asks.

I try to shrug again. My stomach is busy deciding if the bites of cereal I did eat have any right to be there.

"What can I do to help?" she says.

94

"Nothing." That one I know the answer to.

I rinse out my bowl and head back to my bedroom.

I flop onto the floor and lie facedown. No puffin shirt to wear. No idea what to do.

I just know I can't let Cal Carpenter win.

I flip over onto my back. Katherine Johnson is staring down at me. She looks so hopeful.

She would pick herself up. She would have a plan. Maybe it would even involve triangles.

I take a deep breath. Maybe I have another button-down shirt in the closet. I push up off the floor and rummage through the clothes at the back of my closet. Nothing. But maybe . . . I crawl over to my bed and reach for the money sock I keep under it—because no one would ever think to steal a dirty sock.

I count up what I have. Thirty-seven dollars and forty-two cents. That might be enough to buy a new button-down shirt. I'll draw the puffin on if I have to. Because no one else at school wears super-snug button-down shirts. And no one else wears a puffin on their shirt. And I am not like anyone else. It's a trifecta.

I put on an undershirt and sweatpants, stick my money sock and a black Sharpie into an old backpack, since I didn't have time to grab mine before taking off on Friday. Then I yell goodbye to my mom and slip out our apartment door.

The barometric pressure is 30.1 and rising, so I don't take a raincoat. I'm going to be late to school, but I don't care.

I calculate the slope of the hill as I go. Parts of triangles, all of them. When I get to Broadway, I cross the street to avoid the sidewalk near the church's drop-in center for homeless teens, because I don't want to get asked for money. When I get to the store that I hope has button-down shirts, it's not open yet. Definitely going to be late for school.

I sit on the sidewalk and lean against the brick building. The sun is poking its way out from behind a cloud. It's finally warming up.

All of this feels good. To have a plan. To be in the sun. To not be at school.

And, really, who's going to care if I'm late?

The people walking past are my kind of people too. Men and women in suits—and lots of button-down shirts.

I'm tracing the shape of a puffin on the sidewalk when I feel something hard hit my leg. It's a quarter. From a man in a suit walking by.

"Don't waste it," he says.

That's when I realize: The undershirt. The old backpack. Me sitting on the sidewalk.

He thinks I'm one of those kids I try to avoid near the church drop-in center.

Don't waste it. I watch the man as he continues on down the street. Is he going to look back to check? He doesn't, but I can tell he feels all good about himself now, when, really, he threw something at someone and lectured them in the same instant.

And exactly what can you buy for twenty-five cents?

Suddenly, I picture Cal Carpenter as an adult. He's walking down the street in a suit, because by then he'll be wearing button-down shirts since he wants to grow up to make lots of money. Feeling all superior.

Other people are coming. And they'll think I'm one of those kids if they just see the quarter lying next to me, so I shift my right leg to cover it. When the sidewalk has emptied out and there's no one looking, I slip it into my pocket.

As soon as they unlock the doors to the store, I go in and find a button-down shirt that's nice and snug. It's a light green instead of white, but I get it because the triangular corners of the collar are extra-starched. And when I try it on, it's like my neck is being hugged by those triangles. I use almost all of my thirty-seven dollars and forty-two cents to buy it—but I don't need that quarter. Back outside, I take out my Sharpie and start to draw a puffin on my new shirt. I take my time and draw its body first and then its round head with awesome triangular action, but it's all supposed to be very small, and the Sharpie's point is kind of thick.

Again, it comes out looking more like a UFO drawn by a three-year-old.

Oh well. I take a deep breath and put it on. UFOs can fly too, right?

Maybe I'm from another planet and this makes more sense.

But puffins know that for every nesting season, they're going to come back together and be surrounded by hundreds and hundreds of other puffins just like them.

I want to be a puffin.

The wind picks up, funneling between the buildings, and I start walking. I try to calculate the hypotenuses between points. Between a streetlamp and a garbage can. In the incline of the sidewalk. Then I crest the hill, and that thing happens that sometimes happens when the sun is out and you come around the right corner in Seattle.

There in the distance, out in all of its glory, is Mount Rainier.

The mother of all triangles.

Then I make sure to pass the triangle-shaped corner park on Madison, even though it's out of my way.

My mind is still on triangles when I hear a growl. A dog with its teeth bared is a few feet away. Short and squat, with a head and a body that look like they're made for fighting.

I take a step back. "It's okay, doggie." My voice is trembling, but I try to say it good and loud. Dogs listen to loud, right?

I'm about to take another step back when the blanket

the dog is standing on moves, and a person starts to emerge from beneath it. A kid, actually. In a green raincoat.

A kid who was sleeping on the street in front of the church drop-in center I always avoid. Why wasn't I paying more attention?

The kid sits up, looking right at me from under the hood of a raincoat. The kid's eyes are like deep, dark, sad pits boring into me.

I don't think I've ever seen anyone look so lonely.

And suddenly, all I can see are those eyes, and all I can hear is the dog growling, and soon all I can feel are my two feet slamming against the sidewalk.

Because I'm running.

Away.

I'm three blocks away when I realize I've seen that green raincoat before.

The kid who gave me a shirt.

But I keep running.

This time I'm not running from kids who are being mean. This time, I'm pretty sure I'm the one being mean.

That kid gave me a shirt. And I ran away from him.

In between each of my pounding steps, I hear a voice inside.

I'm just as bad as that man with the quarter.

Just as bad as Cal Carpenter.

And when I finally get to the corner where I'm supposed to turn right to go to school, tears are streaming down my face. After all I've gone through this past week, how could I be like them?

I turn left.

Toward home.

Because if I can't face myself, how could I possibly face the kids at school?

LIBBY

MONDAY, MAY 7

RIGHT NOW I'M supposed to be chopping onions for tonight's dinner. Diced finely! Why not just chopped? Do you get more food this way? Or is it just to create more "useful" work for me.

I peer out of our apartment window at the street. I haven't snuck out again since last week's close call, but I'm itching to. Even though I took the bus home, and even though I got out tonight's recipe and the chicken and the onions and the plastic baggies—which my mom's bought jumbo packs of—I can still hear a voice inside me as clear as the bright-yellow double line going down the road. And it says:

It's time to go into the sunset.

The whole world is before you.

And anyone who doesn't think the double yellow line says that should listen better.

Just then, I see my dad get into his car. He's going to

the auto parts store across the river. A thirty-five-minute window! Fifty minutes if his buddy Lou is working today and they start talking. As long as I stay focused, I'll be able to make it.

I pack the index cards I made into my backpack and jog downtown. It's mostly downhill, but I'm still breathing hard when I get there. I just have to pretend I'm doing a few extra warm-up laps in softball.

I check on the index cards that I left around town before. One fell into a gutter and got too soggy to read, but another one is still there. And the second one in the bush is gone! That was the one that said *Rise and shine! You make this world extra-sparkly!* I mean, I know it can get windy here, but what if someone really picked it up?

I want to lie down right now on the nearby bench and imagine the kind of person it might have been, but the clock is ticking and I've got new index cards to spread around. I have to stay *focused*.

I put a new one on the bench, and walk over to check on the *I'm rooting for you* card that was tucked into the edge of the art supply store's display window. It had come loose, so I try to get it tucked back in nice and tight. I should remember to bring a roll of tape next time. Although I probably shouldn't be putting tape on a store window.

Oh. Maybe I shouldn't be putting anything here. Someone is coming out of the store. A lady who definitely seems to work there.

"Can I help you?" she says.

"Oh, no, thanks. I'm okay." I tug the index card free and drop it in my backpack. "I'll just be going."

"Can I see what you just put in your backpack?" Her voice is firm but not mean. Also, her glasses are deep red and speckled with flecks of orange and yellow.

I pull out the index card and hand it to her.

"Who's this for?" she asks.

"Anybody."

"Anybody?"

"You know, anybody who needs it."

She looks from me to the index card.

"Like if somebody gets bullied," I continue, "and they're feeling alone, then maybe this can help them remember that the bully isn't always right."

The woman nods. "I see. Do you have others?"

"Oh, yeah," I say. "I have a whole bunch." I hand her a stack from my backpack and watch her as she flips through them. "Because lots of people get bullied, you know?"

"I know," she says. "I was just on the phone with a friend of mine, and her son is getting bullied horribly at school."

I bite my lip. "I'm sorry. That stinks."

"You know, you're about his age. What would you think if someone started coming to school wearing the same super-tight button-down shirt every day?"

"I don't know. I guess he likes the shirt?"

"It certainly seems so. The shirt has a puffin on it, and

he says that he just really likes the puffin, but it's like he has a death wish."

Puffins. Those are the birds on the cereal box. I'm pretty sure I read that they're called "the clowns of the sea." Kind of like when someone calls you a clown for wearing an awesome rainbow outfit.

I straighten up. "Maybe he just really appreciates puffins. Maybe we all should like puffins."

"Yeah, but sometimes you've just got to go with the flow."

"But—" I press my lips together to keep from saying something disrespectful. Why don't we all just get together and make the *bullies* go with the flow a bit and let people wear what they want to wear?

The lady is looking at the card. "Okay, well, if you want to leave some of these around, I don't see why not."

"Thanks," I say.

I tuck the one that says *I'm rooting for you* back into the edge of the window and then keep walking along the sidewalk. I place the one that says *Stay strong* on top of the newspaper stand. Just two more left, the ones I never found spots for last week.

I perch the one that says *Jump for joy! You're terrific!* in the doorway of the shoe store. Then I look down at the last one in my hand. It's the one that says *Fly free! We're right behind you.* The one that has a V of birds flying off in the sunset.

Wait!

I run back to the art supply store. I burst through the door. "Do you know your friend's address?"

She tilts her head and looks at me. "The one I was telling you about? Sure."

I stare at the rows and rows of fancy art supplies I can't afford to buy while she clicks through screens on her computer.

"Here it is," the art store lady says.

I look at the address. Seattle. I carefully copy it onto the back of my index card—my index card that has now become a postcard!

I look at my drawing of the birds again, and I feel like the card needs something more, so I add: *Because YOU are amazing.* I underline the *YOU*. A lot.

"Thank you so much," I say as I run out the door. I don't have much time left, and I still need to get to the post office, so I run. Fast. I don't care if people are looking at me weird.

"Hi," I say when I get to the front of the line at the post office. "I need a stamp to mail this." I've counted all the coins at the bottom of my backpack, and I have eighty-three cents.

The man nods, much slower than I would think it's possible to nod. "Okay then, little lady." He takes out a big binder of stamps. "We've got lots of stamps to choose from . . ." He's flipping through the binder one page at a time. "And I see you have a postcard. Soooo, you'll be looking for a postcard stamp."

I'm about to scream, *Yes! And please can it be quick!* when I see a stamp at the top corner of the binder. "Wait! Is that a puffin?"

"The puffin stamp is not a postcard stamp—it costs more. You'll want a postcard stamp for what you're mailing."

"No! I want the puffin stamp. Please."

"Miss, I told you that's more than you need."

"That's okay. It is what I want." I quickly count out fifty-five cents and I slide the coins toward him.

He recounts them. One at a time.

Finally, he hands me the puffin stamp. I stick it on the top corner of the card. Then I hustle to the other side of the room to the mail slot. I look at it one last time. "Fly free, fearless puffin," I whisper.

And I push it through the slot.

I sprint home from the post office as fast as I can. But as I turn the corner onto my road, I slow to a stop. My dad's car is still gone, but my mom's beat-up Buick is sitting right there in the driveway. No! She's not supposed to be home this early—and her catching me is way worse than my dad. If he catches me, he yells for a minute but then gets distracted and that's the end of it. My mom is all about follow-through.

I try to stay calm. Maybe she hasn't noticed I'm not

there yet. She doesn't always check in with me when she first gets home. If I can keep her from spotting me from the kitchen window, I might still have a chance.

Please, please be possible.

I cut through the neighbors' yards to stay hidden until I reach the scrappy bushes at the back of our lot. Once I'm even with my bedroom window, I make a break for it.

I'm halfway through when I realize my mom wasn't in the kitchen anyway. Because she's standing right in the middle of my room.

"You *were* sneaking out!"

I try to wiggle back out the window, but it's no use. My center of gravity is already depositing me on the floor inside.

"Rex never drove me crazy like this."

I curl myself into a ball and face the wall. "Rex used to sneak out all the time," I mutter.

"Don't talk back. He's not the one who's suspended, is he? And you! You left the chicken out too. Just sitting there to get warm. What were you thinking?"

I keep my head down. That's a question you're never supposed to answer.

"What am I supposed to do now? You're already grounded." My mom has started walking in circles. "What's the next step? Chain you to your bed?"

She shoves the blinds to the side. "There's your father. You wait till I tell him. Don't you dare go anywhere!"

She leaves my room, but I don't even move. I would have just barely made it in time if my mom hadn't come home early. And what was I supposed to do? Stay here and dice those onions and just be okay with being miserable?

My dad bellows at me as he enters my room. "So you thought you could sneak out while I was gone? You think you can just come and go as you please? Well, you can't. This is my house, and this is—"

"Our house, Wally," my mom says. "And I've already told her that. What we need now is a consequence."

My mom seems calmer now that my dad has taken on the role of huffer-and-puffer.

"Consequences?" My dad paces around my room like I'm not even here. "She doesn't listen to consequences. That's why she snuck out in the first place." He has stopped his pacing to peer out the window. "Hey—there's Wilson Napier!" he says. "I haven't seen him since last fall."

He rushes out of the room, and soon I hear him shout, "Wilson, my man." Wilson Napier has a landscaping business, so of course my dad is excited. So many engines that might need fixing.

My mom sinks down onto my bed. "When I was your age." She shakes her head. "You just don't know how good you have it."

I feel something catch inside me. There's something about her eyes. How they're tugging down at the edges.

"Mom, I left for a good reason," I blurt out. "I'll show

108

you . . ." Because maybe I *can* make her understand. I reach into my backpack and pull out the colored pencils and index cards. "I was—"

"You can't be serious," she says. "Coloring? That's what you were doing? At least be sneaking out to meet friends like other kids."

That hurts. How's a kid with no friends supposed to answer?

I line up the colored pencils next to me.

It's just me and my pencils.

An individual sport.

My mom's staring at me, and I wonder if she feels like crying too.

She looks up at the ceiling. "I don't know what to do with you," she whispers. "No. I *do* know what to do," she says, leaping up. "It's like what your dad says about his engine business. You've got to speak the language they'll listen to."

What is she talking about?

The next thing I know, she's scooping up my colored pencils. "Rex is right. You're always in your own little dream world, and that's not good for you. You've got to grow up. So no more coloring."

"But I need those pencils! They're for school," I protest. I would even write that five-paragraph essay to get them back.

"Well, tell those teachers of yours that your parents are

making sure you learn respect and focus, because *they* sure aren't doing a good enough job of it."

"But, Mom . . ."

She stops on her way out the door. "I'm doing this for you."

Then she shuts the door.

Taking all my future sunrises and sunsets with her.

I crawl into my bed. Pulling the blankets right to my chin. Erasing any signs that she'd been sitting there.

The *Create the world of your dreams* rock is still under my pillow. I squeeze it tight with both hands and curl my body around it.

It's all I have left.

Six impossible words and not a single ounce of hope.

VINCENT
TUESDAY, MAY 8

IN THE MORNING, my mom sits down at the end of my bed. "We've got to figure out a way to get you back to school."

I open one eye and then close it again.

"Personally, I'd start with changing your clothes," she says.

I roll over to face the wall.

"Vincent. Think about it. Things were okay before you started wearing the puffin shirt."

"Things were *not* okay then."

"Well, you weren't staying home from school because your stomach hurt."

Maybe I should have been.

"What do *you* think would help?" she asks.

I look up at my poster. "If I was actually Katherine Johnson."

She swallows and shakes her head. "Are you sure you don't want me to call the principal and see if there's anything else they can do?"

I picture the principal. The way he pats Cal Carpenter on the back every time he passes him in the hall and makes some cool-sounding comment about whatever game Cal just played.

I shake my head.

"Well, something's got to give."

I look at her, and she presses her lips together.

"It's tough-love time, okay?" She clasps and unclasps her hands, like she's trying to convince herself. "You can stay home for a few more days, but you are going to school by Thursday. No matter what, okay?"

I look at her. I'm not willing to nod. Who would agree to walk into their own nightmare just because four school days is too many to miss? Just because her friend June said it was time for "tough love"?

She sighs and slings her bag onto her shoulder. "Vida has jury duty today, so it's just me staffing the store, but I'll try to get home as close to six p.m. as possible. Hopefully, the traffic won't be so bad." She gives me a kiss. "I love you, okay?"

I watch her as she leaves. Is she really going to force me to go to school?

And is she right? Should I be able to just toughen up and deal with it? I mean, it's not like those kids ever actually hurt me. It's not like it's a matter of life or death.

Suddenly, I think about that kid in the green raincoat. Those eyes. How do eyes look that lonely? Did he run away from home? Is that why he's on the street? Living on the street *is* an actual matter of life or death.

I pull the covers up to my chin. At least I have a bed to curl up in. And food to eat. And a mom who cares, even if right now she thinks that "caring" means throwing me to the lions.

I take a deep breath. I've got to get out of bed. Eating my cereal will help.

But when I open the cupboard in the kitchen, there are no boxes left. Instead, there's a note.

No more Puffins. Find a way to get yourself back to normal.

Back to normal?

Back to invisible.

Back to pretending to be someone who's not me.

T

TUESDAY, MAY 8

Family.

Why would anyone miss them?

Thanksgivings filled with arguing.

Uncle Eddie with his homemade cranberry sauce,

getting under my mom's skin.

Pointing out every gap in her logic,

whether about how she bastes the turkey

or her praise of the Pilgrims.

He'd give me a wink

and then stick his thumb

in whatever pie there was.

Somehow the silent daggers she'd shoot from her eyes

bounced right off him.

By the end, my mom's face
was like she had eaten the cranberries
without the sugar.
Every time.
Why would anyone miss family?
Why?
Where's the logic in that?

JACK
WEDNESDAY, MAY 9

THE NIGHT OF the school board meeting, my mom drives me to the town hall down in the valley.

"Did Mr. Sasko say he'd meet you inside?" she asks when she pulls our truck up in front of the building.

"Yes."

It's true. He did say that.

But he also called just before we left to tell me he had an emergency with his wife's mother and he wouldn't be able to come. He wanted me to wait until the next school board meeting to go. But I've got the petition signatures all ready, and what if the next school board meeting is too late?

I look around. All the buildings here in town are so much closer together. No room to breathe.

"Are you sure you don't want me to come in too?" she asks. "I could probably skip this training at the hospital if I absolutely had to."

"No, it's fine. I'll see you after the meeting."

If I tell her about Mr. Sasko, she'll insist on coming in with me, and what the school board needs to see is strength. Strength and competence. It's one thing to be there with your principal. It's a whole other thing to be there with your mom.

Still, I don't think I've ever lied to my mom before. Well, except after Alex's death when she kept asking me if I was okay, and I kept saying I was.

I feel the petitions in my pocket. They remind me that I'm not alone. I've got the whole town with me. Counting on me.

As I open the door to climb out, my mom leans across the passenger seat of the truck and squeezes my shoulder. "Good luck. Your father and I are so proud of you for doing this."

"Thanks." I know my mom is proud. I try to remember exactly what my dad said when he called last night. I'm pretty sure it was *Make me proud, Jack.* Which is different. But by the end of this night, I *will* have made him proud.

I shut the door and stand up as tall as Mr. Sasko does when he says the Pledge of Allegiance. Then I start walking.

The building is three stories and all brick. It's bigger than anything we have in Haycock unless you count the barns, but those don't feel like "buildings" the same way this does.

A man strides past me, a briefcase in one hand, a phone in the other. He doesn't look at me. I take a deep breath and follow him through the door. His shoes are shiny. But that's okay. My boots belong in this building too, right?

It isn't obvious where the school board meeting is right away, but the man heads up a flight of stairs, so I head up right after him. By the time we get to the third floor, I hear other people. A whole lot of them, actually.

It's a fairly big room, and it's already packed. There are reserved seats at a long table in the front of the room, with nameplates facing out. The school board, I guess. Three men and two ladies. They don't look like my neighbors. No one here does. And they're all adults. All of them. Somehow I thought a school board meeting would have kids at it.

I survey the empty chairs. I told Mr. Sasko right before we got off the phone that I'd do my best, so I can't sit in the back. I belong here just as much as the man with the briefcase, right? So I stride right up to the front of the room and take a seat in the first row.

It's when one of the ladies calls the meeting to order that I realize I don't have any idea how this works. What the heck is "approving minutes"? It's like they all speak the same secret language, because they all go through this weird set of lines about making motions and seconding motions. Plus, all of them seem to be set to the maximum level of bored.

Things pick up a bit when a member of the audience raises her hand and asks whether it's true they're considering getting rid of half a foreign language position, and it sounds like that's what most of the audience is there to hear about, because everyone is suddenly talking at once.

The lady in charge of the meeting whacks her metal water bottle on the table loud enough to silence everyone. "The issue of the foreign language position is number three on tonight's agenda," she says.

That settles everyone else down, but all I can think is: *There's an agenda?* How was I supposed to get on that? And they're about to get back to the boring "motions" in the language no regular person can understand, aren't they? They're all set to make decisions for the rest of us hicks.

Just like Ms. Duxbury is trying to do.

And suddenly, all I can picture is the way she pursed her lips and shook her head at Mr. Sasko like he was a child. Mr. Sasko, who has given his life to our school and deserves respect.

My hand shoots up. "Excuse me, what happens when there's an important issue that isn't on the agenda?"

The head lady looks up. "And what's your name?"

"My name is Jack Galenos."

"Isn't it nice that you're here? Is this part of a school project?"

"No, ma'am. This is about keeping Haycock School open."

The lady's expression changes, and I feel everyone looking at me. I've got my John Deere hat on, but no one else here is wearing a hat. Should I not be wearing one?

"Is your principal here with you?" she asks.

I try to keep my voice steady. "Mr. Sasko had a family emergency at the last minute. But he knows I'm here and wishes he could be too."

One of the men on the school board leans back and smirks, and the lady exchanges a look with another school board member. "Okay. You can bring it up when we get to 'New Business' once we get through the rest of our agenda."

I nod, but I don't take my eyes off the smirking man. He's already against us, isn't he?

The meeting goes pretty quick once they get to the foreign language part, and the head lady explains it was just a typo in the proposed budget and no one is getting cut. All the grumbling dies down, and behind me I can hear folks starting to pack up their things.

"Our final item is 'New Business.'" The head lady looks at me. "Why don't you explain what's going on up in Haycock."

The people who were getting ready to go stop their rustling.

I clear my throat. I need to sound the way Mr. Sasko does when he's explaining a complicated math problem. Clear and concise. "We have a great school up on the hill.

It's the center of our community. But we were just visited by a lady from the state who made it sound like we might not get a Small School Grant next year."

"Why is that?"

"She said they're cutting back on how many grants they give out. And they're making it harder to get one, making us jump through all these hoops. Maybe because they think they know better than us. Maybe the state doesn't even trust us enough—"

"Jack . . ." The lady interrupts me, but her voice is soft— and kind of reminds me of Mrs. Lincoln. "Exactly what sort of 'hoops' are they making you jump through?"

"Well, there's a whole bunch of things. But random stuff. None of it was about how well we're learning. I mean, she even complained about our bathrooms."

"What's wrong with your bathrooms?" the smirking man asks.

"Nothing," I say. "They just don't want us to have a girls' and boys' bathroom anymore."

"You mean they're requiring a gender-neutral bathroom," the head lady says. "That doesn't mean getting rid of the other ones."

"But it's a small school—we only have two bathrooms. And it wasn't just that. She didn't like that we don't have any wood chips on our playground, and . . ." I stop when I realize I'm starting to ramble. I didn't come here to argue with them. I try again. "Our school is really important to us. The other students and I collected petition signatures from everyone in town to make sure we can keep our school and make our own decisions. I've got all of them right here. One hundred and sixty-seven." I take the folded stack of paper out of my pocket. "Would you like to see them?"

I walk to the front table to deliver them to the head lady, but instead of saying how impressed she is with the stack of signed petitions, she says, "So why don't you start by just fixing the playground and changing the signs on the bathroom?"

"Because the point is that our school works fine the way it is. We're learning, and that's what's important."

The head lady leans into her microphone. "Do you understand that the point of a gender-neutral bathroom is to ensure that all children, not just those who identify as boys or girls, have a place where they can go to the bathroom? That's why it's a state law. Don't the people in Haycock agree that's important for all children?"

"Sure. But that's beside the point, because our school doesn't have kids like that."

Somebody behind me calls out, "How do you know you don't have any transgender kids?"

I half turn around in my seat. "We can just tell, okay?"

The head lady is flipping through the petition pages. "What exactly do you expect the school board to do about this?"

I'm ready for this question. "Call the state and encourage them to give us the grant again next year, so we can be sure our school stays open."

She nods. "Yes, I imagine you do need that grant, and—"

"Son," the smirking man says, "the only call I'm going to make is to that Principal Sasko of yours to tell him not to send his students to do his dirty work. And that he needs to get his head out of the twentieth century and wake up."

"Mr. Sasko is an amazing principal, and he wanted to be here—but his mother-in-law got sick at the last minute." I shouldn't be yelling, but I can't help myself.

"Jack, I think that it's best that you calm down," the head lady says. "And sit down."

I take my seat. Why did I have to yell? I've got to keep it together. For Mr. Sasko. For Joey. For all of them. "Sorry, ma'am," I say.

"Mr. Stinson here is right." She gestures to the smirking man. "Having a gender-neutral bathroom is now a state law. Mr. Sasko has to follow it."

Another school board member chimes in. "We did it at Pearson Elementary before the law was passed. As long as the single accessible bathroom isn't for specifically girls or boys, you're fine."

"We don't have an extra bathroom," I say. "But anyway, it's not the bathrooms that are the important thing. It's how the state—"

"Well, you can't assume . . . ," the head lady starts.

"Hey! You should listen to the kid!" A man I've never seen before is standing up near the back of the room, shouting.

I catch my breath. This stranger is defending me!

"The whole lot of you are out of line," the man continues. "Of course he doesn't want those trans kids at his school, because the whole thing is gross!"

Wait. That's not what I meant.

"That's my grandchild you're calling gross," an old lady calls from the other side of the room. She shakes a pair of crochet hooks in the air. "You take that back right now. You don't want to see what I do when I'm angry."

"It's freedom of speech!" the man yells back. "And Jack over there is free to say what he thinks too."

"It's not really about the bathrooms," I say.

But no one can hear me. Everyone is talking now, and the head lady is thumping her metal water bottle on the table as loud as she can.

"Settle down," she calls. "I'm adjourning this meeting. Because clearly this is a topic that we're not ready to discuss calmly or to solve right this minute." She turns to me. "It seems to me like there may be a misunderstanding here. It sounds like the state is being clear about its expectations— it's simply a matter of whether you're willing to follow them." She turns back to everyone else. "And those of us with girls on the varsity softball team know that the game starts in ten minutes, so can I have a second to adjourn?"

"Seconded," one of the men on the school board says.

Around me, everyone is standing and getting ready to leave. But all I feel is rage, and I know I have to get out of here fast so I don't erupt and make Haycock School look bad. Even if the school board just stated flat out that my entire town doesn't know what it's talking about and that we're stuck in the wrong century. Even if that guy thought I meant things I didn't say.

As soon as I make it to the stairs, I run down as fast as I can to get outside and wait for my mom. As others start to come out, I make sure my head's held high.

I'm standing tall when the woman with the crochet hooks comes right up to my ear. "You tell that friend of yours that he's a hateful bigot," she says to me. "And if you all want to come for my grandchild, you're going to have to fight me first."

He's not my friend, I want to say, but I don't trust myself to speak.

Then the shouting man himself comes up behind me and says, "You stick to your guns, you hear!"

Suddenly, a man with a notebook and a camera is talking to me. The camera clicks as he takes a picture. "I'm a reporter with the *Falls Gazette*, and I was wondering if I could get a quote from you about your thoughts on the transgender bathroom law. It seems like it makes you really angry."

I don't open my mouth. What is there to say? I've made a mess of everything.

All I can do is stare down the street.

Hurry up, Mom. Please get here soon.

LIBBY

WEDNESDAY, MAY 9

I'VE ALWAYS HATED going with my dad on his little "collection trips." The people who owe him money are always the ones who can't afford to pay. But twenty minutes ago when he told me I was coming with him, all I thought was that at least it'd get me out of the house. Right now, all I can think is: *What kind of person jumps out of her chair to go help shake someone down for money?*

We're standing in some family's kitchen. It's even smaller and gloomier than ours. It's dinnertime, and the guy didn't want to let us in, but my dad insisted. That's one of the reasons my dad likes me to come along—because it's harder for people to say no to you when you've got your daughter with you.

My dad is doing his trademark thing of being super friendly and complimentary, like noting what a nice new slow cooker they have. "Oh, Cindy would love one of those. Libby, don't you agree?"

I nod. Because my mom probably would. But I don't look up at the guy the way I'm sure my dad wants me to. I'm not going to force my dad's point that he shouldn't have bought a slow cooker if he wasn't going to be able to pay to fix his car. How was he supposed to know his car was going to die?

"I just need more time," the guy says. I can hear his little kids whispering from the next room. He sent them away when we first came in, but I can see the older girl's bright-pink leggings through the crack in the door. She starts singing softly. Is she trying to keep the rest of the kids calm?

If I could give her an index card, it would have a tree growing bright-pink heart-shaped apples. And maybe it would have music notes all around it. Like the tree was an instrument. I could even add a squirrel hole in the trunk and put strings across it, like a guitar. I would write, *We're all singing with you.*

But I don't have any cards or colored pencils. I tried to get more pencils from Mr. Cruck at school, but he told me that I needed to be responsible with my school supplies—"because colored pencils don't grow on trees." I wanted to say, *Yeah, they actually do,* but I held my tongue.

Now my dad is putting his arm around the guy like they're buddies. They aren't. "You can have as much time as you need," he says.

The guy looks hopeful. "With no interest?"

My dad's eyes light up like a cat who released the mouse just to snare it again. "Now, how would that be fair?" He gestures to me. "This girl needs to eat, doesn't she?"

They both look at me then. This is where I should call out my dad for what he's doing. Look right back at them and declare I won't take part in it.

But I don't. I can't.

I stand there, staring at my sneakers.

Silent and powerless.

Because he's my dad.

When we're back in the car, I stare out the window while my dad talks. He gets pumped up after visits like this and loves to relive his favorite moments. He gives me a play-by-play as though I wasn't just there having to watch the whole sad thing.

Then he moves on to how his dad would be proud of him, because he always used to tell him to not take no for an answer and how he's good at that now. And how I need to be paying close attention. "Because you can't let folks walk all over you. People always want to squeeze whatever they can out of you. You've got to be strong." He pokes me for good measure.

We turn onto Main Street and drive past the library and the fire station. My dad slows down near the town hall, because there's a crowd on the sidewalk and some of them are spilling into the street.

He swerves around them. "Stupid people," he mutters.

The people in the crowd look all riled up. But not at my dad. They're all focused on a kid in the middle. He's got a John Deere hat, and he's got his chin raised so high that it's like he's daring someone to punch him.

And maybe they're going to—they look angry enough.

Before we pull away, I crane my neck to take one last look at the kid and the crowd.

All these people. Miserable.

So much for creating the world of my dreams.

VINCENT
THURSDAY, MAY 10

ON THURSDAY MORNING—the day my mom is forcing me to go back to school—I wake to find her sitting on the end of my bed. I debate whether I should tie my bathrobe belt to the headboard so she can't make me go. But she just wants to talk.

"I know you said you wanted to be Katherine Johnson," she starts in. "And I was just wondering, do you feel uncomfortable as a boy? Is that what's making you miserable at school? Although you seem pretty miserable here at home too. And I don't want—"

I look at my mom. "It has nothing to do with being a boy."

"Okay. I just didn't want to assume what you were feeling on the inside, and you know you can always talk to me . . ."

I don't have a clue what she's going on about. But she looks relieved.

"Oh, Vincent, I just want to be the best mother to you that I can be." She leans down and kisses me on the top of the head. "I want you to be happy. If it helps, you can stay home again one more day, okay?"

Which is what I wanted.

I think.

So why don't I feel happier?

After she's gone, I sit at the kitchen table, trying to rearrange the letters of *Cheerios*, *Special K*, and *Raisin Bran* to try to spell *Puffins*. But I'm missing the *u* and the *f*'s, and nothing else has the same sweet, crunchy taste.

Maybe Mom's right. Maybe I am making things worse for myself. I've got plenty of shirts that nobody would notice.

Except that once you've figured out who you are, can you really forget about that? And how long can you last trying to pretend you're someone you're not?

But how long can anyone take being lonely?

I think of that kid on the street with the lonely eyes. I squeeze my own eyes shut. Here I am moping around with three different breakfast cereals. I bet that kid didn't even *have* breakfast. I'm incapable of surviving at school *and* I'm a thoughtless monster who runs away—actually runs away—from a kid who is hungry and sleeping on the street. I'm worse than that guy who threw the quarter at me. At least he thought he was trying to help.

One stupid point in space.

Totally helpless.

Totally useless.

If my point didn't exist, would anyone even care? And my mom doesn't count. Two people can only make a line together. They can't make a three-dimensional shape. They can't form a triangle.

Part of me wants to crawl back into bed, but I'm sick of being in bed. Instead, I crawl under the kitchen table. And I sit there, hunched over, the tiniest, most worthless point in space in the whole gigantic universe.

After a while, I hear the mail lady down in the apartment lobby. She seems to love slamming all our metal mailbox doors louder than you'd think possible. The couple times I've seen her, she's always looked really happy about it too. Maybe you don't feel so worthless if you make noise.

When she leaves, everything settles back into silence. And I think that I'm not like the mail lady—I'm more like the mail shoved into those little boxes, all on their own. Sad, boring rectangles, just waiting to be picked up.

But what am I waiting for?

I let out a long breath. I don't know.

So maybe I should stop waiting. Maybe I should do something.

Something big is overwhelming. But maybe something small?

Like I'm totally capable of getting the mail.

I grab the extra key for the mailbox and unlock the door. That mail doesn't have to wait in its box all lonely anymore.

No one is in the lobby, and I hustle down the stairs to unlock our mailbox. Bottom right. At the ninety-degree angle of a triangle that's formed if you divide the block of mail slots diagonally in half.

I pull out the small stack of mail. Just some bills. But less lonely bills than before.

Back in our apartment, I deposit them all on the kitchen table, and that's when I see it: a very *non*-bill thing hiding between two larger envelopes. I pick it up.

It's a drawing.

Of a sunset. With birds flying off into it. And the words *Fly free! We're right behind you. Because YOU are amazing.*

I read the words again.

Because YOU are amazing.

Who is this from? I flip it over. Someone has handwritten my address. Handwritten. With writing that's completely unfamiliar. In the upper right corner where the return address would be, it just says *Libby* next to a small heart. The postmark says Vermont. Even though I don't know any Libby in Vermont. Even though I don't know any Libby in any state.

And there on the stamp is a puffin.

I flip the card back over to read for a third time what a stranger named Libby wrote to me.

Fly
free!
We're right
behind you.
Because
<u>*YOU*</u>
are
amazing.

I know Katherine Johnson never cried in the movie, but that doesn't matter. It's the giant kind of sobs that come, and I'm not sure I'll ever be able to stop. Like when you sit in a parked car when it's pouring, and all you can see are sheets of water against the glass and all you can hear are the thundering raindrops around you.

Except this time, the thundering is inside me.

I do finally stop crying, and I take a few shuddering breaths. As the last few tears dry on my face, I study the postcard again.

Then I start pulling out of the cupboards the things I need to make a bunch of sandwiches.

I know a bigger something that I can do.

THURSDAY, MAY 10

Peko's fur is warm.
Maybe that is
all I need.

Six hours until the drop-in shelter meal.

All I need.

One meal.
One Peko.

My stomach disagrees.
I pull my knees up tight.

So many strangers.
Walking by.
Driving by.

Not caring.

But then.
That boy.
There he is again.

Coming back.

VINCENT
THURSDAY, MAY 10

I SEE HIM. I can tell it's him from far away because the same dog is asleep at his side. The dog lifts its head and stares me down, teeth bared, but I am determined to keep walking forward.

The boy looks at me too. Or girl. I'm not sure. Short hair. I guess he's a boy. But as I get closer, I see eye makeup—you must care a whole lot about makeup if you manage to wear it while living on the street.

Before I can chicken out, I sit down—but not real close because the dog is still watching me. I place the shirt and bag of sandwiches between us and give them a nudge in his (or her) direction.

"Thank you for the shirt," I say.

I haven't looked directly at the kid, but I sneak a peek now. Those are some wide eyes. Maybe I shouldn't have sat down.

But now the kid's looking at the bag.

"Those are sandwiches for you," I say. "I made turkey and tuna, because I didn't know what kind you liked."

I don't have to say anything else. He (or she) opens the bag and starts eating. Turkey first. Then the tuna.

"I guess you like both?" I say.

The kid pauses midbite and nods. "Thank you."

"My name is Vincent."

The kid swallows. "Thank you, Vincent."

"What's your name?"

He (or she) doesn't say anything.

"Sorry," I say. "You don't have to tell me."

But then the kid says something so quiet I can barely make it out. "What?"

"T," the kid says again. "My name is T."

I want to ask if T is a boy or a girl, but it seems rude. Still, I have a lot of questions. "Did you run away from home?"

T looks away, but then nods.

I watch him (or her). Are *him* and *her* the only options? What's an in-between?

T's hair is going every which way. Maybe it once was a buzz cut, but it has clearly been growing out for a while.

Before I can stop myself, I've blurted out, "Are you a 'he' or a 'she'?"

T shrugs.

"You don't know?" I say.

T is still looking down the road. "I don't think I'm either."

"Neither? That's a thing?"

T shrugs again.

"I mean . . . that's fine. But what do you do if you're not a 'he' or a 'she'? How does someone talk about you? What are they supposed to say?" I stop myself, hoping I'm not being totally rude.

T lets out a long breath. "Maybe 'they'?"

They? Them? Really? *Their* hair? *Their* dog? *Their* sandwiches? I don't think I've ever said "they" before about just one person. But maybe it's like there's a whole group of people in there. Maybe I should have brought even more sandwiches. T still looks hungry.

"Isn't it hard to live on the street?" I say softly.

T pulls their knees up to their chest again.

"You want more sandwiches?"

Then T looks at me. And nods.

I swallow and scramble up. "I'll be back in half an hour."

I bring back two of each kind of sandwich, and when I sit down, T's dog doesn't bare its teeth at me.

T eats slower this time. When there's just one sandwich left, T looks at me, their hand on the dog's head. "Is it okay if I feed this to Peko? She's hungry too."

I nod, even though I'm kind of annoyed that I just took the time to make that sandwich so nice, and it's about to disappear into that scruffy dog's mouth. But when I watch

T feeding her, I'm embarrassed to have even had that thought. It's like watching an old couple doting on each other, completely oblivious to the rest of the world. And Peko doesn't look nearly as mean and scruffy after she's been fed. She even rolls onto her back, belly up. T makes a sound that might have been a giggle and rubs her belly. "Thank you," T says again.

"Sorry I ran away from you before," I blurt out. "I was having a bad day."

T keeps rubbing Peko's belly.

"But *you* probably have lots of bad days," I say, glancing at the people crossing the street to avoid us.

T doesn't look up, and I think they haven't heard me, but then they finally say, "What makes you think I have bad days? I might have lots of good days, you know."

"Oh, I mean . . . I didn't mean . . ."

"At least no one's telling me how to live my life."

"That's more important than having a home?" I ask.

T doesn't say anything.

I was rude again, wasn't I? "I'm sorry."

They shrug and switch to rubbing Peko under the ears. Maybe life *would* be better with a dog.

We sit there for a long, long time. Peko goes back to sleep.

"Do you know that puffins can flap their wings four hundred times a minute?"

T looks at me.

"And they can swim underwater the same way. They're like rockets. With feathers."

Since T still doesn't say anything, I keep going. "And they can survive out in the ocean on their own. Just bobbing up and down on the waves and hunting for food. For eight months—that's a really long time."

"What do they do after that?" T asks. "After being out at sea for so long."

I swallow. "They come back together. They meet at their nesting area. With all the other puffins."

T looks away, and so do I. I can guess what we are both thinking.

Where are all of T's puffins?

Where are all of mine?

I stand up and tell T goodbye. "I'll come back later," I add. "And I'll bring more sandwiches. Tomorrow too. For both of you."

T just keeps looking away.

"Okay?"

T nods slightly.

"Okay," I say.

THURSDAY, MAY 10

That kid comes back again.
Talking more about puffins.
Flapping four hundred beats per minute is fast.
But flying away
doesn't solve *every*thing.

He wants advice.
They keep shoving him in lockers.
How's he supposed to go back to school?
I don't know what to say.
At least no kids ever shoved me in a locker.

But he keeps sitting there.
Waiting.
Waiting.
Waiting.

"Defensive stance," I finally suggest.
"Like in basketball."
He looks at me
like he's never,
ever,
ever
watched a basketball game.

I stand up.
Legs wide.
Arms open.
"Like this."

I pull my arms back down.
I miss basketball the most.

"Or you could do it like this."
I put my hands on my hips.
"Show yourself
you can be strong."

Peko is looking up at me.
Confused.
Why would I stand up?
The drop-in center
is still closed.

But the kid,
his eyes are wide.
"Do
you
know,"
he says slowly,
"how many
triangles
you're making
with your body right now?"

JACK
THURSDAY, MAY 10

AT SCHOOL TODAY, Mr. Sasko and Mrs. Lincoln asked how the school board meeting went. It was hard to look at them. Mr. Sasko had advised me to wait until he could come, but of course I didn't listen.

Finally, I tell them. "I don't think I did a very good job at the meeting. I wasn't a great representative of the school."

"Oh, Jack, don't be hard on yourself," Mr. Sasko says. "You were brave to go and stand up for all of us."

I grimace. "They called us backwards. They don't have a clue how good this school is, and I—"

"That's their loss," Mrs. Lincoln cuts in.

They both ended up patting me on the back, telling me I'm great. But they weren't there. They don't know.

When I get home from school, I drop my backpack on the porch and sit in one of my mom's rocking chairs. Her shift at the hospital goes late every night this week, and my dad won't be home until the weekend. I listen to the birds chattering in the bushes on the side of our house—it's like they're just as excited about spring as my mom is.

From across the ridge, I hear the high-pitched whine of a chain saw. I remember hearing a chain saw just like that—maybe the same one—when I was waiting with Alex that day.

I remember that no matter how hard I yelled for help, I couldn't be as loud as that chain saw.

And I didn't have a cell phone, so that meant that I had to leave his side to call 911. That I had to run away from my brother so I could use the landline in the house.

The 911 woman had told me to stay with him until they got there, and I nodded even though right then I was standing in our kitchen in the middle of a pile of spilled chips—and not holding my brother's hand like I should have been. She gave me a bunch of advice and told me that under no circumstances should I move him. And that someone would be there soon.

I called my mom's cell phone right after that, but it went straight to voicemail. Which made sense, since she and my dad were helping our neighbors the Burbanks with their haying. I found the landline number for the neighbors and called them, but of course no one picked up.

And the whole time, through the window I could see our barn and knew that Alex was lying beside it.

I couldn't spend any more time on the phone. I ran back

to him. I was so careful not to move him, just like the 911 people had said. "Alex, can you hear me?" I said. "I'm right here. Help is coming. They said they'd be here right away. They'll be here soon. I promise."

He was breathing. I know he was because to me, his breaths were louder than any other sound. The birds. The wind. That whiny chain saw across the ridge.

And that's when I noticed the blood that was quietly pooling behind his head. What had that 911 lady said? If there's any bleeding, apply pressure with a cloth and don't let up till help comes.

I ripped my shirt off and flipped it inside out to get to the clean side. But how could I get to the back of his head without moving him? I did my best to gently slip my hand with the shirt under his head. The orange shirt instantly turned deep red. I put my other hand on his forehand. Just like a steady vise grip, right? No moving. No more losing blood. With every part of me, I hoped that this was what I was supposed to be doing.

But then it was just me and my two hands trying desperately not to shake, and Alex and his head that kept insisting on bleeding.

And where was the ambulance? Where were the police? Where was anybody?

For fifty-one minutes.

I wanted to run back in and call 911 again, but I couldn't leave Alex.

I shouted, *"Help! Help! Help!"* until my voice gave out.

And then in the silence that followed, I realized that Alex's breathing wasn't the same anymore.

All I could think to do was to start singing his favorite song to him. The song our mom used to sing to us at bedtime. *On the loose to climb a mountain. On the loose where I am free.* My voice broke every time I got to the part about how you *only have a moment and a whole world yet to see.*

When my parents came back from the Burbanks' field and saw us, they started running—faster than I'd ever seen them run.

But it didn't matter by that point. The 911 people had taken forever. It reminds me of what my uncle Sid and his buddies always say about why they need to have guns: *When seconds matter, help is minutes away.* It this case, fifty-one whole minutes.

◟◡◞

The whir of the chain saw stops, and I brace my hands against my knees and take in a long, shuddering breath. That's when I realize that there's another sound. A low hum. On and off. It's my phone vibrating in my backpack. My mom got it for me after Alex died, and she insisted I carry it with me at all times.

When I take out my phone, it's a text from Sturgis:

Dude. You're in the news! You gonna be all famous!

It's like everything else around me disappears. He's

included a link to a news article, and I click on it. I'm holding my breath. Because there I am in the photo. It's definitely me. Definitely in front of the town hall. And definitely surrounded by those horrible people. The headline:

FOR TRANS STUDENTS IN A RURAL AREA, GENDER-NEUTRAL BATHROOM LAW MEETS RESISTANCE.

I swallow. As if it were even about that—or that simple.

I start skimming the article—it's obvious they quoted a bunch of those angry people who thought I hated transgender people. And I don't hate them! I just don't know any, but that's not a crime.

At least they included that quote from me about how there *aren't* any transgender people in our school. Hopefully, that will make it clearer.

At the bottom of the article, the first comment is from Sturgis. HEY! That's my bro Jack Galenos!!!

Sturgis. I bet he didn't even read the article.

I scroll back to the top. That reporter guy said he was with the *Falls Gazette*, right? But this isn't the local paper. This is the state paper. The whole *state* is reading this?

My phone starts buzzing as I scan the article, but I can't handle Sturgis right now.

I stare at the porch floor. I need to convince myself that having lots of people read about our little school might help. Because Ms. Duxbury can't push us around the same way if everyone is paying attention.

But with my picture? Seen by people all over the state? It's too big.

My phone is still buzzing. How many texts can Sturgis send?

But it's not from Sturgis, and it's not a text. It's a message request on one of my social media accounts from someone I don't know.

> Would you do an interview with us? We want to
> understand how you can know that no one in your
> school is transgender.

After the name is the call sign for a radio station I don't recognize. I close out of that message and suddenly realize it's not the only one. I have a whole screen of message requests from strangers.

> Shame on you. I will pray for your soul to
> give up its bigoted ways.

> How dare you assume you know what is in
> someone's heart.

> Good for you for telling off those . . .

I turn off my phone as quick as I can. I'm shaking. To keep myself from hurling the phone into the woods, I jump down from the porch, pick up a rock, and throw it as hard and as far as I can. It clears the barn roof and breaks through the leaves in the trees beyond with a smack.

Every part of me aches to go back in time. To not have to worry about any of this. To have Alex here again, and our family whole again. I imagine Alex running out in that big yellow tie-dyed T-shirt of my mom's that he always wore, flapping his arms like he was a butterfly. *Let's fly away!* he'd say, and we would.

I look up. I hear something. The chirping of a bird, loud and fast. Different from any birdcall I've ever heard before. Like a cry for help.

I follow the sound past our woodpile, and then I realize where it's coming from. The far side of the barn, where we store the ladder. Where I try not to go. But now I have to go there again. My legs feel wobbly. The grass is long back there, because I've refused to mow it since that day. But my dad doesn't complain. He doesn't talk about it, but he gets it. He doesn't go over there either.

The grass is damp, and it soaks my pants as I step through it. The chirping is louder, and it's not coming from the trees. It's coming from the ground.

And then I see it. A wounded baby bird in the grass. Its wing is broken, splayed out to the side. The bird is flapping its wings in a panic, but instead of flying, it's only sinking deeper into the long grass.

I look up. Did it fall out of a nest? There are no trees overhead. Could it have crashed into the barn? The barn doesn't have windows to trick it and make it think it can fly right through. Maybe it hit something in midair?

I freeze. The rock I threw couldn't have done that, could it?

It was going in this direction, but what are the odds?

But what if it did? My whole body is shaking now. So much that my teeth are chattering. What if me getting angry means that this bird is going to die?

I can't let that happen.

I pull my phone out of my pocket and turn it back on. I ignore all of the notifications and look up how to take care of an injured bird. The first step is to call animal rescue, and I click on the phone number, but I get their voicemail message, saying that they won't open again until nine tomorrow morning.

The next thing the website says is to build a nest for it, to help it stay warm. Just like the mama bird would do.

I promise the bird that I'm coming right back. And I force my wobbly legs to run to the house. As quick as I can, I find a small cardboard box and grab the other supplies listed on the website. Then I run back, kneel down, and add some of the softer strands of long grass into the box.

And then, with gloves on, I ever so gently scoop up the bird. Willing my hands not to shake. Even though the bird's body is so light I can barely feel it. Willing my hands to be just what the bird needs, to do just what it needs, I wrap it in one of my mom's dish towels and place it gently into its new nest.

I might be imagining things, but it seems calmer once it's in there.

I breathe.

The bird breathes.

Maybe it can tell that it's being taken care of.

Maybe it can tell that it's not alone.

I close my eyes. The long grass is all around me.

Maybe.

VINCENT
FRIDAY, MAY 11

LAST NIGHT, I stared at the postcard for a long, long time before going to sleep. Could it be true? Could I really be amazing just the way I am?

But why would having a stranger tell me that make it true?

Except that that postcard got me to do what I should have done all along. If I hadn't been so scared.

What if I'm amazing like it says? *Especially* if I stop being scared of who I am.

Katherine Johnson wasn't scared of who she was. Even if she was different from the people around her. I look up at the poster. The way she's got her eyes up. The way she's got her hands on her hips, just like T said.

I can do that. I can convince myself that I'm stronger than I feel.

Just like T said.

Amazing, just the way I am.

Just like the postcard said.

I get out of bed, pull on my bathrobe, and practice. Hands on hips. Someone wants to stuff me in the trash to see if they can break me? Why don't they try? I'll climb out of that trash can and walk away.

I look down at myself and check out the fabulous strong triangles I make with my arms when I put my hands on my hips. I've got this.

I march into the kitchen and stand in front of my mom. "I have an announcement."

My mom has been on her laptop, and she slams it shut like the screen just caught on fire. "An announcement," she breathes. She places her hand on her heart, then switches to holding her coffee mug, and then switches again and clasps both hands together tight. "Okay. I'm ready."

"I have a plan for going back to school."

"A plan," she says slowly. "For going back to school." She doesn't seem as excited as I thought she'd be.

"Yes," I continue. "I'm not going to school today, but that's only because of certain obligations I have."

"Obligations," my mom repeats.

"But next week I will go back. You have my word."

"Vincent," my mom says quietly. "Are you okay?"

Am I okay? She's asking if I'm okay now? When I finally have a plan?

"Mom. I'm more than okay. I'm great! No! I am amazing!"

"Vincent, you don't have to go back to school if you're not ready."

"No! I'm ready. That's what I'm saying! Because—"

"Because if there are people at school who aren't treating you right, maybe we can see if there are alternatives. Homeschooling for a while. It'd be tricky, but I think you could work in the back office at the store. Or maybe you could switch schools."

What?

I don't know what to say. Homeschooling. Where I could just be by myself. Learning on my own. Never having to see Cal Carpenter again.

"Think about it, okay?" my mom says. "I just want what's best for you."

All morning, I pace around the house and think about it. I already use an online math program that could work for homeschooling, even if it wouldn't be the same as with Mr. Bond. And I could do a research project about the space race and Katherine Johnson's role in it. That could count for both social studies and science. Just learning. No other people.

But then I'd really be a point in space.

I flop onto my bed, take the postcard out from under my pillow, and read it for the forty-sixth time.

An *amazing* point in space.

But still. Is that enough?

At eleven thirty, I make two turkey and two tuna sandwiches. I cut them each diagonally to make eight perfect triangles. T definitely deserves triangles. I put them in my lunch box. Then I head out the door.

T is lying in the exact same place near the Sunshine Center. Peko is curled up behind T's head, sleeping on their big red backpack. She looks peaceful until she hears me, and she raises her head, teeth bared. But then she sees the lunch box, and a salivating tongue replaces the teeth.

T rustles in the sleeping bag. It's one of those cocoon bags, and at first all that's peeking out is T's hair. It's the same dark color as mine. Finally, T emerges, at least part of the way.

"Hi," I say.

T nods at me. I wonder if T thought I'd come back.

"I brought you more sandwiches." I push the lunch box toward them.

"Thank you," T whispers.

I'm not sure if I should look at T as they start to eat the sandwiches, or look away to give them space. I settle on watching the dog. "I had come up with a plan," I say. "I was going to go back to school and be all confident and bring you two sandwiches every morning on my way. But now . . ."

T stops chewing, I think waiting for me to continue.

"But now, my mom says maybe I don't have to go—maybe I could do homeschooling from her store."

T is silent. And I realize they've stopped eating mid-sandwich.

"Your mom loves you," T says.

I look at T and swallow. "Yeah, I'm lucky, aren't I?"

T's response is to go back to eating the sandwich.

"It's just that there's something about the homeschool-ing thing that doesn't feel right. Like I'm giving up. Because I had a plan."

T turns to Peko and feeds her the rest of the tuna sand-wich. "Then stick with the plan," T says.

"But I don't know if it's a good plan."

T looks out down the street. "There's only one way to find out."

They say it with such certainty.

"Running away was *your* plan, wasn't it?" I ask.

T doesn't turn to look at me, but they nod.

"Do you think it was a good plan?"

This time T doesn't nod. They just keep looking off down the side street, toward where the traffic on Broadway is rushing by.

"I guess you couldn't find out until you tried it," I say.

I watch T. I'm sure this is where I should leave and stop my pestering, but I can't help myself. "So, if you're a 'they,'" I blurt out, "does that mean you were born a boy, but really you're a girl?"

T shakes their head. "Then I'd be a 'she.'"

"But . . ."

"I don't fit into either the boy box or the girl box. I'm just me."

I swallow and nod. "Not 'just,'" I say.

"What?" T says.

"Not you're *just you*. You *are* you. No 'just' about it."

T shrugs and starts to slip back into the sleeping bag. "Thanks for the sandwiches."

"Maybe it would be okay if you called home," I blurt out. "Maybe they've changed their minds?"

But T's head disappears.

‿◌‿

When I get home, I sit down at the kitchen table. My mom's laptop is still where she left it when she rushed out this morning.

I switch over to her chair and open up the laptop. Had she been looking up information about homeschooling? Or other schools?

I see an email from her friend June. The subject is: THIS is why you should homeschool him. But instead of there being a list of reasons, there's just a few lines.

This article is from our state paper, but it happened around the corner from me. You need to protect Vincent from having to deal with this kind of thing. And I know you're going to say that things like this don't happen where you live, because Seattle is so progressive. But Vermont is supposed to be too. You just can't predict how people are going to react.

I scroll down. The article's headline is FOR TRANS STUDENTS IN RURAL AREA, GENDER-NEUTRAL BATHROOM LAW MEETS RESISTANCE.

But I'm not transgender. Did my mom tell June she thinks I am? Was this because I said I wanted to be like Katherine Johnson? That doesn't mean I want to be a girl!

I start making a mental list of all the male role models my mom has. Vincent van Gogh is number one. Banksy. Christo—that guy who wrapped things up. And Andy Warhol. Does admiring those men make her want to be a guy?

I'm not trans, and I'm not gay, and I'm not a girl. It's like T said. I'm just me.

No, I *am* me.

I scroll down to see the article. There's a picture of a boy surrounded by people who clearly seem to hate him.

I start reading. According to the headline, he's the one doing the bullying, but that picture says otherwise. He looks so alone.

I keep reading. The boy Jack seems pretty clueless. Like, does he really think he can tell who is transgender and who isn't? I thought I could figure it out with T, but T had to explain it to me. It isn't that hard to understand if you're willing to listen.

What would this kid do if he was face-to-face with someone who is transgender?

For some reason, I can't stop looking at that picture. The way the boy's keeping his chin up even though he's surrounded. Does he think he's amazing? Or is he just pretending to?

I stare at the picture for another long moment.

I want to tell him things.

And suddenly, I'm riffling through our closet off the hallway, where we cram random stuff. I push aside polka-dot duct tape, an old map, and a broken umbrella, until I pull out what I was looking for.

An index card.

T

SUNDAY, MAY 13

Two.
Could that be enough?
I try to pretend it is.
One friend who is not a dog.
Plus one friend who is a dog.

I don't know.

Logic would say that two
is more than nothing.
But it still isn't much.

JACK

MONDAY, MAY 14

THE FIRST THING I did was hide the bird in my bedroom closet. The internet said to keep it inside to help it stay warm, but I couldn't let my dad find it when he was home for the weekend. He'd just tell me to "be a man" and that dying birds and animals are a part of nature. Aren't we hunters? Why was I letting a bird poop in my closet?

But it would die if I left it outside. It's still really cold at night up here in the hills. And, yes, we're hunters, but we aren't going to get a dinner out of this bird. It's too small. And it wasn't supposed to get hurt.

On Friday morning, I called animal rescue. I had told my mom I was sick, to avoid having to go into school, so I could be home to make the call. And, yeah, she's a nurse, but I never pull stuff like that, so she believed me.

The man who answered asked me a number of questions: about the bird, about its injury, about what I've done so far. But when there was a pause and I was ready for him to explain how they were going to save the bird, he said, "I'm sorry. We're super understaffed right now and don't have the resources to help. But you're doing all the right things. Just keep it warm, be careful not to give it too much water, and hope for the best."

That was it.

I hung up before I could yell at him.

Because they're no better than those 911 people. Worthless. Of course I needed to do it myself.

That was three days ago, and I've barely left my room or the bird since. It helped that I did actually get sick with a sore throat and slight fever. Nothing serious, but enough that I didn't have to work much to convince my mom to let me stay home today.

I set up a lamp in my closet and surrounded the bird's box with blankets and sweatshirts and the entire contents of my sock drawer. A nest within a nest.

The bird never moves much, but I tell myself that it knows it's hurt and it's focusing on healing. Of course, it does chirp incessantly. I've been playing the latest Imagine Dragons album extra-loud to cover it up.

This morning, my mom stops in my room before leaving for work. "Are you sure you're okay staying home alone?"

I nod. "I'm fine."

She doesn't look convinced. "You haven't been yourself. I'm worried about you."

I tug the covers up. "I've been sick."

She studies me. "I hope it's not all those terrible messages getting to you. No child should ever be on the receiving end of hate like that."

I shrug. "I'm all right," I say.

Even though I don't feel anywhere near all right.

"Promise me you won't touch that phone while I'm gone."

I swallow. "I promise."

She nods and then kisses me on the top of the head. "Okay."

My mom hasn't said much about the article itself, but my dad sure was proud. I heard him on the phone with my grandfather, bragging about me the whole time. "I'll send you a copy of the article," he said. "You've got to see the determination in his eyes. Our very own David taking on Goliath. Mark my words: he'll be the one to come out on top." And even though I was sick, he actually came and sat next to me on the couch, putting my feet on his lap like he used to when I was little. But for some reason, the more he insisted on reading the article aloud, the more uncomfortable I got with all it said. And I had thought making him proud was what I wanted . . .

After I hear my mom pull out of the driveway, I open my eyes and look out the window. I can only see sky, but it's full of the small repeating puffs of clouds that mean rain is on the way. It'll be good for my mom's garden. The bit of rain we got the other night wasn't nearly enough. She's been waiting for this.

The Imagine Dragons album ends, but before it starts over with the first track, it pauses. It feels like an extra-long pause, but then I realize it's not.

It's an extra-silent pause.

Where are the bird chirps?

I flip over and prop myself up on my elbows to look at the bird.

It is so still. Too still.

My hand reaches for it automatically. Gentle fingers on its delicate little body.

Cold.

Dead.

Horror rises up inside me like vomit. I should have known this was going to happen. I should have prepared myself.

But I didn't. And it doesn't matter how feverish I am. I'm running downstairs. Outside. Trying desperately to keep down all the things inside me that need to stay down.

Why?

Why did it have to die?

Why can't I ever keep anything safe?

I collapse on the bench near the garden and put my head between my knees.

When I finally sit back up, I see one of those fuzzy

caterpillars dropping from the trees right in front of my face. It's black with a blue stripe and white dots, and long spindly white hairs, like whiskers. It's spinning slowly as it descends.

I watch it. Completely fixated. I start to breathe normally again.

Alex would know what kind of caterpillar this is. He was always pointing out woolly bears, and it took me forever to realize he wasn't talking about an imaginary friend. The summer he died, it seemed like caterpillars were raining from the sky—they were everywhere.

The caterpillar finally touches down on the ground and starts crawling away. Alex would have followed it, and I want to too. To try and keep it safe so it can become a butterfly. But who am I fooling? I'm no good at protecting things.

For the Halloween that turned out to be his last, Alex had wanted to *be* a butterfly. But there was no way my dad was going to buy him a costume like that. So instead, I suggested my dad get him a Superman costume. I figured Alex would like the cape. But he didn't. I still remember the way he looked when he opened up the package and saw that costume.

"That's not a butterfly," Alex wailed.

"But Superman is so cool," I said. "He's so strong!"

"A butterfly!"

"It's just a costume," I said, which of course didn't help. Alex was still crying.

Finally, I said, "You know, Clark Kent is like a caterpillar that becomes a butterfly when he's Superman. People think he's boring, but really he can fly!"

Alex nodded and wiped his eyes. "People don't know."

I put my arm around him. "Yeah. There's what people think, and then there's who he really is."

And even though I know he wanted a butterfly costume more than anything, he wore the Superman costume that Halloween and didn't say another word about it. My dad didn't even know he had been upset.

I stand up when I hear a car. It's Sharon, the mail carrier, in her Jeep.

She shoves a stack of mail into our box and calls out to me. "Hey, Jack! Hope you're feeling better! Someone sent you a card addressed to you at school, but when Mr. Sasko said you were home sick, I figured I'd bring it to you here."

I force myself to wave. "Thanks," I manage to say. And then I watch her drive away.

I stare at the mailbox. It doesn't matter if I ignore my cell phone. It looks like the angry messages have found a new way in. Part of me wants to burn the whole mailbox down just to show them they can't get to me. Except that, really, it's that I can't take it. I can't take any more.

The people who think I'm being mean. The people who *are* being mean and think I agree with them. I know I'm supposed to stay strong, but I can't.

But I have to go get whatever it is. I can't risk my mom or dad finding it instead. This is my problem, not theirs.

I force myself to walk down the driveway.

I force myself to open the mailbox.

I force myself to take out the stack of mail.

There it is. Right on top. A small card. It's an index card, actually. And smack in the middle of it is my name—*Jack Galenos*—and *Haycock School, Haycock, VT*.

I won't flip it over to see what's written on it. I won't let them get to me.

But then I notice tiny writing next to the stamp. There's a bird on the stamp. A puffin? I can barely make out the writing because it's so small, but I'm pretty sure it says *Puffins rule*.

What is this?

I can't stop myself. I flip the card over. The writing is even smaller on this side, with so many words crammed in.

Dear Jack,
    I know what it's like to feel all alone. So I'm sorry if you feel that way too. But I don't agree about the transgender stuff. There might be people who are but don't say. Because you can get

bullied. Getting bullied for who you are is awful.

For example: This kid T had to run away from their own family. Now T lives on the sidewalk next to a place called Sunshine Center. It sounds nice but in Seattle the sidewalk is not a sunny place. I was scared of T at first. Then we talked. You don't know what someone's going through till you sit next to them.

So, I am reaching out from across the country to let you know I'm sitting next to you too. No one should have to be alone.

Sincerely,

Vincent

I'm sitting at the base of the mailbox. I don't know when I sat down. And I don't know why everything is blurry when I look around.

I touch the neck of my T-shirt. It's wet.

And then I realize: tears are running down my face.

Because I am simultaneously understanding two things . . .

That I have been alone.

And that I don't have to be.

I keep going back and rereading the same sentences: *Getting bullied for who you are . . . their own family . . .*

Did I sit there and just let it happen lots of the times when Dad bullied Alex?

I lie down in the grass. Massive gray clouds are rolling in from the west, and they stretch from one end of the sky to the other.

You don't know what someone's going through . . .

Did I know what Alex was going through? Did I listen?

Or did I just listen to my dad?

I picture Alex and his stomachaches, all alone in his room.

The tears slide off my cheeks and into my ears. Filling me up from the outside in.

⟡

Before the rain starts to fall, I bury the bird on the far side of the barn.

A little mound amid the long grass.

My voice barely works, but I sing "On the Loose."

Then I promise to make things right.

LIBBY

MONDAY, MAY 14

AFTER SCHOOL, I come home on the bus just like I'm supposed to, and I say hi to my dad in the garage just like I'm supposed to. I actually laugh for real at his joke. It's new, and my dad smiles when he tells it. "Where does a general keep his little armies? In his little sleevies!" But then my dad goes back to ignoring me and trying to convince some guy named Carl to bring him his lawn mower, so I head inside.

As soon as I get into the kitchen, I start getting dinner ready just like I'm supposed to. My mom isn't getting home until late, because she's going out to dinner with her friend, so tonight I'm not just prepping ingredients—I'm supposed to cook all of dinner. All of the creamy herb mushroom chicken. For my dad.

I open the package of mushrooms. It's a shriveled type, because evidently that's what the cooking show people say is best. I put them in a colander in the sink and discover they're really hard to clean. How can anybody tell the difference between what's dirt and what's withered mushroom?

I stare at the mushrooms. If a person's soul just kept withering away day after day, would it make a sound to show it was going to disappear forever? What if it was too small to make a sound? What if it was only as big as a shriveled mushroom?

But it couldn't disappear without sending out some kind of sign, right? Even if it's small. It's about whether or not you're listening. Like in *Horton Hears a Who!*

I pick up one of the mushrooms and hold it to my ear. Is this mushroom trying to tell me something? Too bad I don't have elephant-sized ears.

Just then, my dad walks in. "Can you believe that guy said my prices are too high? What does he think—" He stops and stares at me. "What are you doing?"

I drop the mushroom, and it skips across the floor. "Nothing," I say.

"You should be getting dinner ready." He picks up the mushroom and squishes it between his fingers.

"I mean, I am."

My dad stares at the mushroom. "Have you ever seen anything so gross?" He laughs. "Chop the rest up tiny so I don't have to look at them when I'm eating. Who even gave stuff this gross the right to exist?"

Then he flicks it into the trash.

Like his flick is the decisive stroke from an all-powerful being.

As if.

As soon as he walks back out to the garage, I dig through the trash to find that mushroom. I'll rescue it and paint its portrait so it will live forever! Uneaten! It will never be digested by those who don't understand it!

I run into my parents' bedroom to rescue something else. I pull a chair into the closet and climb up to see the upper shelves. There, in all their glory, are my colored pencils, my glitter glue, and my index cards. I gather them into my arms.

Some things aren't worth listening to.

Some things—like the cry that a mushroom (or a soul) makes when it's flicked into the trash—are.

After I've made a whole lot of fabulous mushroom cards, I jump up.

I need to put them out in the world now!

But when I look out the window, the sky is getting dark and it's starting to rain. If I take them to town, they'll get soaked. But if they stay here, my parents might find them and throw them away, and I'm not sure I could take that.

Wait! They don't have to get soaked! In an instant, I'm running to the kitchen and grabbing every one of those blasted Ziploc bags.

I'm drenched by the time my backpack and I make it downtown, but each little index card is safe and dry inside its own personal Ziploc bag raincoat. I didn't even wait for my dad to leave. I didn't have to. He was so focused on some phone call that he didn't look up when I slipped out the window and right past him. What kind of person would sneak out into the rain to leave index cards around town for nobody in particular?

A person who doesn't have a choice.

The rain has switched to torrential, and new streams are starting to run down my face and back. I leave my cards in the usual places: in the bush near the dentist's office, tucked into the side of the art supply store's window display (which is harder to do with a baggie, but I make it work), and in the decorative planter outside the bank.

Mostly, I'm keeping my head down to keep the rain out of my eyes. There are a few other people around, but they're the kind who have rain boots and big umbrellas and aren't sopping wet inside their sneakers.

I have one more index card left. I look up from the sidewalk to try to find one more good spot. Across the street is the town hall. Was it a week ago that we drove past and that crowd was outside? I still can't stop thinking about that boy in the middle of everyone—and how hunted he looked.

When there's a break in the traffic, I dash across the street. My last index card definitely needs to go in front of this building.

I jog over to inspect some large planters when I realize someone is standing at the top of the stairs near the door. A person as wet as I am.

And then they turn around.

It's that kid I couldn't stop thinking about.

JACK
MONDAY, MAY 14

I ALMOST DIDN'T write the letter, because this town and the people in it are my whole world, and they've been counting on me. And this letter to the school board could be the opposite of making a lot of them proud.

Except that it's the truth.

When my mom came home this afternoon to check on me before going back out to do a few errands, I convinced her that I needed to get out of the house, that I was healthy enough to go with her, and that staying cooped up was messing with my head.

Which it was.

I tucked the letter in the inside pocket of my jacket, and when we parked in town, I told her I'd meet her back at the car. That I wanted to go for a walk first.

"In the rain?" she said.

"Yeah," I said. And I pulled up my hood and walked in

the opposite direction from the hardware store, where she was headed.

I walk up the stairs to the town hall. But it's after five and the door is locked. There's no meeting tonight to keep the place open late. The overhang from the roof juts out just enough to protect most of me from the rain. Could I leave the letter right here in front of the double glass doors? No. It'd get wet. But I have to deliver it. I can't wait another day. There has to be a regular mailbox somewhere. Or at least something I can put it in to protect it.

I look around.

And at the bottom of the stairs I see a soaking-wet girl. Holding out a plastic baggie.

"This is for you," she says.

"What?" I say.

"I know you," she says slowly.

I shake my head. I don't know people outside of Haycock, and no one from Haycock would be in a polka-dot sweatshirt or rainbow-striped leggings.

"No, I remember. You were standing right on the sidewalk over there last week with a bunch of people. And I read the article in the newspaper too."

She saw the article. Of course she did. And I bet she has an opinion of me even though we've never met . . .

"Can I ask you just one thing?" she says. She's coming up the steps. She's still holding the baggie out to me. I can see paper inside it. Is she delivering a letter too—except she was smart enough to protect it from the rain?

"I don't mean this is a bad way. But"—she pauses—"do you feel better after you bully someone?"

I stare at her.

"I mean, like, do you feel stronger?" she says. "Because sometimes, I wonder if . . ."

"I wasn't trying to hurt anyone."

"Really? Then what were you trying to do?"

I look down at the card in her hand. It has a picture of a mushroom on it. "I was just trying to keep things the way they've always been."

"Yeah. I guess you wouldn't want things to change. Unless things were bad for you. Then you'd *really* want things to change, right?"

"Um . . ."

"Like, for example, how would you feel if you had to live in a room filled with someone else's dirty socks?"

I look up at her. "Wait. What?"

"Wouldn't you want things to change then? Even if things might be good for you, and your room isn't filled with someone else's socks. But for other people, it's like . . ."

She's looking at me expectantly.

"A room full of socks?" I ask.

"Stinky socks, specifically. Left all over the room to show who's boss. If that was your room, you'd want to change that kind of situation."

"Yeah, I guess so." Is it as simple as that? It seems like a lot of "for examples" are coming at me lately. From that kid Vincent about his friend T. And now from this kid. Does that mean I need to listen better?

She nods and holds out the baggie again. I peer at the card inside. It's a drawing of smiling mushrooms. Through the wet plastic, I can make out a few of the words around them: *beautiful . . . have a fungnificent day . . .* "What's a fungnificent day?"

"Just take it." She puts the bag in my hand.

"But what is it? Does that say 'fungnificent'?"

"Yep. I mixed *fun* and *magnificent*—and added a mushroom."

I look more closely at the card. "Or lots of mushrooms."

"Yes! Then there's more fungnificence for everyone."

Every mushroom is beautiful, and so are you. I hope you have a fungnificent day!

"Why are you giving this to me?"

"Because maybe you need a fungnificent day."

"Do you have more cards like this?"

She shrugs. She does.

"What do you do with them?"

She looks away. "I mailed one across the country once, but mostly I just leave them around. I don't know for sure that anyone's ever gotten one. Except for you, that is. You're not going to throw it in the trash, are you?"

"No—but the one you mailed—who'd you mail it to?"

"Just some boy."

"You said on the other side of the country. Like in—"

"You wouldn't know him." She waves her hand. "So, tell me what you're doing here now."

"Nothing," I say.

"Don't lie. It's much harder to have a fungnificent day if you lie."

I smile. "Just trying to deliver a letter too."

"For who?"

"The school board," I say. "But I don't know where to leave it where it won't get soaked."

"You know, baggies can be reused," she suggests.

I look down at the mushroom card again. "Good thinking."

I step back to where I'm fully protected by the overhang and carefully take the mushroom card out of the bag. I can see it better now. Every mushroom has a face. Most are happy, but some look thoughtful. Their eyes are made of glitter.

"Thank you," I whisper. "I like these mushrooms."

She bites her lip.

Then I tuck it into my pocket and take out my letter.

"You know that bag still has bits of glitter from those mushrooms," she says quickly. "Is it the kind of letter that goes with that mushroom glitter?"

Something catches in my throat. I nod.

She's looking at me square in the eye. "Are you sure?

Because you couldn't have put the things you said in that article with mushroom glitter."

"This is different." I swallow. "I promise."

She takes the baggie and holds it open for me, and I fold the letter and seal it inside. Then I stoop down to carefully shimmy the bag with the letter through the space under the door.

"Good," she says.

I stand up.

"I should get going," she says.

"Me too," I say.

"See you."

"See you."

And then we do that awkward thing of both leaving in the same direction.

When we're waiting to be able to cross the road, she looks at me. "What's your name?"

"Jack Galenos." I pause. "What's yours?"

"Libby Delmar."

There's a break in the traffic, and she takes off at a run. "Nice to meet you, Jack Galenos!" she calls over her shoulder. "Stay fungnificent!"

I can't help but smile as I watch her yellow sweatshirt flapping behind her like the wings of a butterfly.

T

MONDAY, MAY 14

I made the mistake of thinking I could tell my mom.
I made the mistake of believing her
all those times she said she'd be open-minded.
That she'd never judge.

I made the mistake of listening to her
tell me I needed to go to someone
who'd help me "get over it."

That it was a phase.
That it was a problem.

That I needed fixing.

VINCENT
TUESDAY, MAY 15

FOR THREE WHOLE days, I considered the idea of switching to homeschooling or going to another school. But it felt like giving up on a math equation right when you've figured out the formula to solve it.

My mom wasn't convinced when I explained my hands-on-hips plan, but she doesn't understand the power of two strong triangles on either side of you. Yesterday she must have talked to every single one of my teachers on the phone. She talked with the principal and the guidance counselor too. "I just want your first day back to go as smoothly as possible," she told me.

And I don't know. Maybe she's right that a two-pronged approach is best. Because if you've got two prongs and then you connect them, you know what you get?

Something that's a whole lot like a triangle.

So I did my laundry. Washed my replacement puffin shirt. And I was ready for the morning.

Mom must have been happy with me, because there was a new box of Puffins cereal for breakfast.

She barely noticed that I left early so I'd have time to see T before school.

When I get to the Sunshine Drop-in Center, T is still sleeping. I put a big bag with cereal and milk next to them. Plus another bag with sandwiches for lunch. Peko licks my hand as I add a spoon and bowl to the pile.

I don't want to wake T up, so I pat Peko on the head to try to tell her to not lick the bowl and that I'll be back after school. Then I keep walking.

The closer I get to school, the more nervous I get. Especially when I spot Cal Carpenter and Zachary Wilkins outside the main doors. My mom told me that they both had in-school suspension for a couple days last week. Which might make them hate me even more. But do they hate me? Or do they just get bored and need a laugh? They should try watching clips from the late-night comedy shows. I can always hear my mom giggling through the wall when she has one on.

I look down at my shirt. The UFO/puffin looks a bit more on the alien side after having gone through the wash, but it's the principle that counts. I'm wearing it. And it's tucked in, snug as spandex. Super Vincent.

I walk closer. Right up to where Cal and Zachary and all of their friends are joking around. And then I stand there waiting.

"Look who's finally back at school," I hear Zachary call.

"Did it take you a week to stop crying?" Cal says, laughing.

But I am ready.

I put my hands on my hips. And I feel those power triangles activating, because suddenly I'm speaking just as loud as they are.

"I know you must like puffins as much as I do, but I'd like my shirt back."

"Oh my gosh, you guys, look," Cal says. "He's wearing the same kind of shirt, but . . . wait. Did you *draw* on that shirt?"

I keep my hands on my hips. "I did. I like puffins."

Zachary puts his hands on his hips. "I did," he copies. "I like . . ." He bursts out laughing before he can finish.

I can feel my triangle arms starting to waver, but I take a deep breath and keep them firm.

I keep my eyes up, just like Katherine, and I stare at them. They keep laughing. But somehow when the bell rings and everyone starts to funnel inside, they funnel along with everyone else and disappear into the school. I still have my hands on my hips.

And I feel . . . okay.

Homeroom and science go fine enough. Ms. Jacoby has me doing makeup work in the back of the room. Cal and Zachary aren't even in class. I hear someone say they're in the guidance office, that they got called down during homeroom.

But they are very much in PE, and if they got some kind of deep talking-to that made them question their life choices, they aren't showing it. Unless they're questioning whether they can be even more competitive during baseball drills—which we're "getting" to do because it's not raining for once.

Cal zings the ball faster than I've ever seen a person zing a ball. And the way Zachary is swinging the bat around makes me want to take even more time with my warm-up laps. I'm considering whether they should take the whole period, but Ms. Lemmick is watching, so I finish staggering the rest of the way and take a position in the outfield.

No, I don't have to be scared. I don't have to feel bad. I don't have to feel like I'm less than them.

Right there in the outfield, I do hands on hips. And even though the ball never comes to me, I stay that way for the whole period. And I feel better!

Plus, Ms. Lemmick even puts her hand on my shoulder when we're heading off the field. "That's the spirit, Vincent. It's good to have you back."

But the locker room isn't nearly as big as the athletic

field, and when we're changing back into our clothes, I hear Cal and Zachary snickering near me. "I like puffins!" one of them says. The other laughs.

I gather up all of my Katherine Johnson courage and turn to them. I try to block out the open lockers just waiting for me to be stuffed into them, and I force my hands back onto my hips. I take a deep breath. "I *do* like puffins. It's true!"

They look at me like they want to do some locker-stuffing, but they pause, and I wonder if doubling my width with power triangles has them confused.

Then Lucas, our security guard, shows up out of nowhere. "Hey, Cal. Hey, Zachary. What's shaking?" He gives them a fist bump.

"What are *you* doing here?" Cal asks.

"Oh, just wandering." He smiles. "You know?"

He never looks at me. He doesn't have to.

Either way, I am free.

My mom was right. Two prongs are better than one.

‿6‿

After school, I run to see T. "I did it," I yell as soon as I come around the corner. "I made it through the day! Hands on hips is like a superpower!"

T looks up at me. Maybe even smiles a little.

"You must have felt it when you showed it to me, right?" I say. "Why aren't you doing it all the time?"

T's hint of a smile goes away. They look away from me, down the street.

"You've got to try it again. Here," I say. "Stand up."

Maybe I should have asked how T's day was first. Maybe T isn't in the mood for shouting and jumping around.

But hands on hips is so powerful that it has to work for T too. "Please?" I say. "You can sit back down afterward. I just want you to try it again."

T looks around. The only other person on the street is a man on his cell phone, walking away. When he turns the corner, T shifts the sleeping bag to the side and stands up.

It's when T gets to their full height that I remember that T's like two whole feet taller than me. I've never been friends with someone this big before. "Okay, just like you showed me. Wide feet, hands on your hips. All strong like. This is activating superpowered triangles at your side, right? And then"—I add this on because it's what happens when you've made it through a school day feeling decent—"you survey your domain, and you say to yourself, 'I am me, and that is awesome.'"

I'm looking up and down the street, imagining the whole street, my whole route to school, the school itself, all as my domain. And I'm thinking that, really, if a scrawny kid who was obsessed with puffins appeared in front of me now, I'd be totally excited to be his friend, so maybe this whole "awesome" thing isn't that far off. Even though it just came out of my mouth without permission.

And then I hear it: T's voice next to me.

"I am me, and that is awesome."

I turn, and T's hands are on their hips.

"How does it feel?" I ask.

T looks down at me. But as soon as T meets my eyes, the puff goes out of their chest and they shake their head.

"No."

"No?" I say. "That's not a feeling."

T sinks back to the ground, pulls the sleeping bag around their legs, and nuzzles Peko behind the ears.

I sit down next to them. "What do you mean, 'No'?"

"I mean, 'No, it's not that easy.' I'm really glad it worked for you, but that doesn't mean it'll work for me."

"Why not? Why can't it work for you?"

"It's different."

"How? Why?"

T finally looks at me. "Because every day, *you* go home to your mom who loves you."

Right.

We sit in silence for a long while. Peko goes to sleep against T's leg.

"Do you want to come home with me?" I suddenly blurt out. "You could meet my mom."

T shakes their head. "But thanks for breakfast and lunch." T turns to me. "Were those puffins this morning? That cereal?"

I smile. "Yeah, what'd you think?"

"You might be onto something."

I nod. "I'll bring you more tomorrow."

"You don't need to."

"Yes, I do." I put my hands on my hips. "Some puffins are better than no puffins."

"Thanks." T lets out a small smile. "They sure are."

JACK

TUESDAY, MAY 15

AT THE END of my letter to the school board, I said they could submit it to the newspaper as a letter to the editor. So first thing in the morning, I check the paper.

"How are you feeling, honey?" my mom says as she scrambles us some eggs. "Think you can go to school today?"

"Yeah," I murmur as I skim through all the letters that have been published. It isn't there, but it could show up any day now. I wonder what will happen when my dad finds out. When my friends find out.

I watch my mom as she stirs the eggs around. She's already in her scrubs for work. Today's are covered in bright-pink flowers. She's so good at taking care of people. "Do you think we let people be who they are?" I ask.

She chuckles. "Listen, I don't think we usually have a

choice. What I'd give for your dad to have a job where he wasn't gone all week. But you couldn't force him to sit inside for eight hours if you tried."

"But what if . . . ?"

"What if what?"

I take a deep breath. "What if a boy doesn't want to do boy things? Or doesn't always feel like a boy? Or even . . . doesn't feel like a boy *or* a girl?"

My mom puts down her spatula. "Did you turn your phone back on, Jack? Are you letting those angry people mess with your head?"

"It's not the angry ones. It's the nice ones." I swallow the lump that just showed up in my throat. "And I think they might be right."

My mom's eyes change. They look . . . hungry. When she opens her mouth, what she says is: "Tell me more."

And over our two plates of eggs, I tell her about how at the school board meeting the man who was trying to stick up for me sounded mean and petty. Then I tell her about the postcard from Vincent and about his friend T who had to run away from their own family.

I even tell her about the bird.

"I wish the bird could be back in the sky," I say as my mom draws me into a bear hug. It feels good to have her strong arms around me tight. Like I'm in a cocoon.

"Alex," I whisper into her shoulder. "Alex wanted to be

a butterfly." My whole chest feels like it's going to explode. I push to get the words out. "What if we had let Alex be a butterfly?"

My mom pulls away to look at me. "What are you talking about?"

"I want to find his drawings. They're in the attic, right?" I stand up. "Why didn't we hang any of them up?"

"Jack, are you sure you want to go up there?" she says.

But I'm already bounding up the stairs.

The air in the attic is cold as I search. I finally find the boxes of Alex's stuff in the far corner, where you have to crawl on your hands and knees to keep from hitting your head. And then I find a box of his drawings. I lay them out one at a time across the attic floor. Alex with butterfly wings. Alex with glitter. Butterflies with glitter. Even some ducks with glitter.

I turn when I hear a noise behind me. It's my mom. She kneels next to me and leans over one of the butterflies.

"Why did we never hang these up?" I say.

She shakes her head and bites her lip. "Your dad," she says. "He wasn't a fan."

I swallow. "But what if something's the right thing to do? Even if he doesn't like it?"

My mom looks at me and then looks away and lets out a long breath. "If it's the right thing to do, then you do it."

"But . . ."

My mom finishes my sentence for me. "But I didn't, and I wish I had. I was too interested in keeping the peace with Dad, I guess."

I nod. I sure get that.

"Still, why wouldn't a mother hang her son's drawings on the fridge so he can see how proud she is of him?" she continues. And this time, when she looks at me, there are tears in her eyes. "Because it never occurs to her that it'll be her last chance."

Her words land deep inside me. I bite my lip. "I have to tell you something else."

My mom takes my hand. "Okay."

"I wrote a letter to the school board, apologizing. Saying that I get now why we need gender-neutral bathrooms everywhere. Because everyone should get to be who they are." I look down. "And I asked them to print the letter in the newspaper."

My mom doesn't say anything for a long time. She just sits there holding my hand in hers, her eyes on Alex's drawings. Finally, she says, "I always knew you were brave, Jack. But I'm so glad you're this kind of brave."

I release the breath I've been holding. "Thanks, Mom."

She squeezes my hand. "Anytime."

I keep my eyes on the floor. "Dad isn't going to be happy about it, is he?"

She takes a deep breath. "I'll call him and talk to him. It might take him a while to digest it, but we've got time."

I nod. If I'm going to stand behind the words in that letter, I'm going to need to be willing to be brave again and again.

I look at Alex's drawings. And we might as well start now. "Don't you think it's time we hung some of these up on the fridge?"

My mom bites back a smile. "You know? I do."

✍

I get to school early and find Mrs. Lincoln standing on a chair, hanging up construction paper flowers. "Jack! You're back!" She calls into the hall. "Mr. Sasko, Jack's here!"

Mrs. Lincoln climbs down off her chair. "I'm glad you're feeling better. We were going to send work home but decided to let you focus on resting."

"Jack!" Mr. Sasko says, coming into the room. "We missed you! How are you feeling?"

"I'm okay, but I have a lot to tell you . . ." I look at both of them. "I've been thinking about everything. First of all, that article made it sound like I said things that I didn't."

"It's pretty common for articles to have small mistakes," Mr. Sasko says. "Once the newspaper said I was ten years younger than I actually am. I wouldn't worry about it."

"That's not all," I blurt out. "I think we should change the bathroom signs after all. So there isn't one for girls and one for boys."

Mrs. Lincoln shakes her head. "You don't have to give

up, Jack. We'll find a way through, to do the things we know are right for our school."

"But that's just it. I think it's the right thing to do. I even wrote a letter to the school board about this and said they could publish it in the paper."

Mrs. Lincoln's eyes go wide. "You wrote a letter to the school board? About this?"

I nod. "We think of our school as a safe place for kids, so why wouldn't we want to make it even more welcoming? And we actually don't know how everyone feels on the inside. What if we just wrote 'Bathroom' on each of the doors?"

"Jack," Mrs. Lincoln starts. "I'm not sure . . ."

"We've been upset about being forced to do things *we* don't want to do," I say. "But if someone doesn't feel like either a girl or a boy and they're expected to use that bathroom every time, aren't we forcing *them* to do something they don't want to do?"

Mr. Sasko sits down in one of the youngers' blue plastic chairs, his knees poking out at weird angles. "Jack." His voice is soft. "You know some people will be upset with us."

I look up. *Us*, he said. *Us*.

"I know," I say. "But I think that's okay."

Mr. Sasko looks at the mural of our school. "Change is always hard at first. And it doesn't help when the messenger has to act so superior," he says. "Ms. Duxbury—"

"She had no respect," Mrs. Lincoln says, jumping in.

"No respect for how much of our heart we invest in this school."

"No. She didn't. But it's not about her," Mr. Sasko says. "You're right. We *are* the beating heart of this school." He pauses. "And because of that, we're always going to do what makes our kids feel safe."

"But we've always—"

"I know." Mr. Sasko shakes his head. "But just because change is hard doesn't mean it's wrong." He puts his arm on my shoulder. "It takes courage to see things in a new way. And it takes even more courage to speak up and help others to see it too. Jack, I look forward to hanging your letter on the bulletin board as soon as it's published."

I stand up tall. "Thank you, Mr. Sasko."

My whole body is vibrating with his words as I go to my cubby. And in it I find a card. An index card with drawings of lots of bees—except for a big empty spot in the middle. There's an arrow pointing to the empty spot. I flip over the card, and in huge uneven handwriting it says:

From Joey. School isn't the same without you.

I smile as I switch between looking at the front and the back. It's perfect. *Thank you, Joey.*

And what are the odds he'd use an index card?

LIBBY

WEDNESDAY, MAY 16

MRS. ECKER HAS never been this excited about an art project before. Instead of the random coloring pages she usually passes out—using only the washable markers, of course—she's holding a stack of handouts to her chest like they're winning lottery tickets and she'll never have to sub again. "We have been asked by Principal Hecton and a representative from the Historic Mill Society to help out with this year's Historic Mill Commemoration Day! What I have here"—she squeezes the stack tighter—"are line drawings of some of our town's most famous historic buildings. And we get to color them in! Of course, using only historically accurate colors. And I'm told they'll decorate the walkway leading to the fireworks!"

Across the room, Danielle Fisher squeals and exchanges excited faces with Adrianna. The middle school girls' softball team plays a home game that afternoon every year, and everyone comes. I know. I've been looking forward to being in it since third grade. Not just playing in it, but winning it with a home run and having the whole town want to carry me around. And then watching the varsity games in the evening with the rest of the team (maybe still on their shoulders). By the time of the fireworks that night, it'd be officially the best day ever.

So much for that.

Mrs. Ecker hands me a photocopied drawing of the old paper mill that still sits down by the river.

"And to get that historically accurate look," Mrs. Ecker is saying, "instead of using our usual washable markers, this time we'll be using colored pencils!"

Colored pencils!

Because mine are gone. They went into the trash when my mom finally got home Monday night after my dad had been yelling at me for hours.

When Mrs. Ecker finally gets back around to my seat, she's about to just give me a gray one, because that's the color the paper mill is, but I point to the sky. "But don't you think the sun should be rising over the mill? Wouldn't that be symbolic?"

She looks into the can of colored pencils like doling out too many would give away too much of her power. But then she nods. "That could be nice, I suppose," she says, and she reaches in and pulls out yellow.

"But for a sunrise to look realistic, I'd need orange and red too. And hasn't the sign for the paper mill always had blue letters?"

She eyes me but pulls out the colors. "Just make sure it's historically accurate."

"I promise."

I run my finger along each of the pencils. Even if I'm just going to be coloring a building gray, I can still imagine.

I pick up the gray and draw an entire flock of geese flying away in a V within the walls of the mill. I start filling in the rest of the walls with gray when Mrs. Ecker circles toward my seat, but I still know they're there. Even if no one else does.

That's the thing, isn't it? Why do you need other people's approval to feel good about yourself? Like it doesn't really matter that my index cards never made a difference. What matters is that I made them, right?

Mrs. Ecker is behind me now, inspecting my work. I hunch over my paper and color the whole wall a dark gray. After a long moment, she moves along, saying, "It's good to show respect for the way things have been."

Is it? What if things haven't been fair? What would this mill that's been in our town for a hundred years say? That this is how it's always been and I should give up trying to hope for something better? That no matter what I do, I'm still going to somehow end up like my dad?

Because what's a few index cards compared with decades of bullying?

My coloring is starting to slip outside the lines, but I don't care.

But maybe if I did care, things would be better. Maybe if I stayed inside the lines, and did a better job of staying focused when people tell me to do things, and only used washable markers, and happily prepped dinner for my mom every night, and always found my dad's jokes funny . . . then things would be better. Because maybe my parents aren't even the problem. Maybe I'm the problem.

∽

When I arrive at homeroom for snacks and attendance, Ms. Dixon calls me over to her desk. What did I do this time? Did Mr. Cruck find out about all the index cards I "borrowed"? Do I have to go to the principal's office? If my dad gets called back here again, he'll explode. I'll explode. Principal Hecton might explode.

She hands me something, but it's not a regular note from a teacher or an office slip. It's an envelope with a stamp.

A puffin stamp.

It says *Libby Delmar*, and it has the school's address.

But who would . . . ?

I tear the envelope open to find a folded-up piece of notebook paper that still has the edges from being ripped out of a spiral binding.

Dear Libby,
    I wanted to ask you this when I saw you at the town hall—did the boy you sent a postcard to live in Seattle? Was he named Vincent? Because if it was, then he got it. And then he sent me a postcard too. It'd be wild if it was the same person.
    Also, I really like those mushrooms!

Thanks,
Jack

I read the letter over two more times. Vincent sent Jack a postcard?

I look again at the puffin stamp on the envelope. But how?

I flip back to the letter. Jack left his phone number at the bottom.

My hand shoots into the air. "Can I go to the bathroom?"

Ms. Dixon pauses taking attendance long enough to wave me away. "Make sure you sign out."

With the letter in my pocket, I hustle to my locker, grab my phone, and slip into the girls' bathroom.

Yes! It was Vincent! I text from inside one of the stalls. This is Libby, I add.

My thumbs hover over the keys. There are so many things I want to type at once that I don't know where to start. Mostly, I want to send a drawing of a person's brain exploding into rainbows.

Because what are the odds?

VINCENT

WEDNESDAY, MAY 16

T IS AWAKE when I stop by with more Puffins cereal and sandwiches. "How are you?" I ask.

T shrugs. I can tell they try to smile when I set down the food, but there's nothing convincing about it. The dark circles under T's eyes are a lot bigger. There must be a limit on how many days someone can sleep on a sidewalk and still feel okay—and it's already been a long time.

"Are you sure you don't want to come home with me?"

T shakes their head.

"What about finding a homeless shelter?"

T gestures to the church.

"I mean, one where you can spend the night too. Not just get food in the evening."

"I'm okay."

"You don't seem okay."

T doesn't say anything.

"Are you sure you don't want to call home?"

"You should get to school. You're going to be late."

⌒

I can't stop thinking about T as I walk the rest of the way to school. What do you do when you want things to change for someone but hands on hips doesn't work? When you can't figure out the solution?

What if there *is* no solution, because their family has convinced them they don't love them, so it doesn't make sense to call home?

T was right. I barely made it to school on time. And when I walk into class, there's something waiting on my desk just for me. A note from my math teacher.

I open it before even sitting down.

Vincent,

I'm starting a geometry club, and I'm wondering if you'd like to be part of it. It'll be small (so far, I just know of one other student who's interested), but I think that's okay. We can meet in my classroom during lunch. Let me know if you'd like to join us.

Mr. Bond

I sink down into my seat and trace the imaginary lines that connect Mr. Bond's name with the words *one other student* and *Vincent*. A triangle. A lunchtime one. Like a delicious grilled cheese sandwich cut diagonally.

Proof that things *can* change.

I fold up the note and look around. A new feeling starts to spread through me, warm and bubbly. I don't care if everyone else is talking to everyone else. I don't care if my second period is PE. I don't care if Cal Carpenter is never going to give me my original puffin shirt back.

I am going to be me. And I am going to be okay.

And I'm going to try to figure out a way to help T be okay—or at least more okay.

And the path forward just happens to be paved with triangles.

LIBBY
WEDNESDAY, MAY 16

I DON'T GET on the bus after school. It's like there's a whole lot of fizzy soda inside me, and if I have to listen to Adrianna and Danielle, I'll explode. I keep taking out the note from Jack to read it again. Vincent actually got my postcard! And he thought about it enough that it made him want to write a postcard to someone else. That means that impulsive, mistake-making me did something positive.

I start walking, but this time it's in the opposite direction of our apartment. It's toward 7-Eleven.

As soon as I go through the jingling door, my mom eyes me—and not in a friendly way. When the last of her customers—an old man buying seven cans of soup—has paid, my mom turns to me. "Why aren't you going straight home?"

"I need to talk to you," I say.

She cracks open a roll of nickels for the cash register. "About what?"

This is where I need to say that what I do with my colored pencils is important. That just because it's different from what she does doesn't mean she has to attack it. That I am a sprout shooting up through the concrete, and it's time she gave me some space and sunlight.

But there's something about the way my mom's mouth is fixed in a tight line. What comes out of my mouth is this: "Would you like me more if I was still on the softball team?"

My mom looks up from the coins. "What are you talking about?"

"Nothing. Forget it."

My mom puts her hand on mine and gets in my face. "No, I'm not going to forget it. What do you mean by that?"

"I mean . . . it's just that you used to come to my games and cheer me on, but now it seems like I'm just in your way. I mean, I know you take care of me. But do you even like me?"

"What a silly question." My mom goes back to getting the nickels out of the roll and moves on to a roll of dimes. Eventually, she says, "Let me tell you something—back in my day, there wasn't room for liking. It was about surviving." She gestures to the aisle of canned soup. "My mom tried to protect us. When my dad didn't have a job, we had to eat that soup every night, because that was the food we could get. When was the last time your dinner was canned soup?"

"Mom, that's not what I—"

"When was it?" she presses.

I look down at the counter. "I don't know. A long time."

"You mean never. I have never served you dinner out of a can," she says. "But I spent years eating that soup. The meat was gross little slime balls, but I didn't complain. That's just how it was."

That's just how it was. She says each word like it's been carved in stone.

The door jingles. She's looking at me. Her eyes are red. "When I grew up, I was sure another way had to exist," she says quietly. "They wouldn't make cooking shows with fancy mushrooms if it didn't."

"Mom . . . ," I start, but then I stop. She's looking right past me at a new customer.

"All set?" she says, nice and loud, and I can tell it's time for me to leave.

As I head for the door, I pass the soup and picture my mom eating slimy balls of meat. And never complaining.

Outside, the sun is bright. Part of me wants to go back in time to when she was a little girl and tell her that someday she'll be cooking chicken just like the lady on the cooking show. That things can change. That things can get better. I want her to be able to imagine all that's possible.

Suddenly, I'm pulling out the last index card I made before my colored pencils went in the trash. Where I wrote *IMPOSSIBLE* in giant letters across the top half in gray and black but then crossed it out and wrote *I'm possible* in the colors of a sunrise.

I stare at it, and then I flip it over and write on the back:

I wish I could have given this to you when you were a kid. Thanks for making dinner every night.

Love,
Libby

And then I tuck it under the windshield wipers of her Buick.

JACK
THURSDAY, MAY 17

WHEN I GET to school, Sturgis comes up to me, a football under his arm. "Dude. What's gotten into you?" he says.

"What are you talking about?" I say. Even though I know exactly what he's talking about. The newspaper printed my letter today.

"Come on, man." He knocks me on the shoulder. "You wrote a letter to the fancy-pants school board saying you were sorry. Now you think changing the bathroom signs is a good idea?"

I look away from him. "It's probably always been a good idea. It's just that we didn't realize it."

Sturgis stares at me, his lips tight. "What happened to my old buddy Jack?"

I shake my head. "Same Jack."

Sturgis rolls his eyes and tosses the football up in the air. "No. You've changed, dude."

"Maybe. But maybe that's not a bad thing." I pause. "You know one thing that hasn't changed?" I grab the football out of his hands. "That you won't be able to catch me."

I take off with it tucked under my arm, and I reach the field before Sturgis. He still looks mad, but we play football like we always do. And even though he hits harder than normal, that's okay. I know where I'm going. And I drag him right into the end zone with me.

⟋⟍

At the end of the school day, Joey and I stay around shooting baskets together for a while. Mostly, I'm lifting him up to dunk while he chants his name on behalf of the imaginary crowd.

When I'm about to pick him up for yet another dunk, Mr. Sasko comes out of the building.

I call to him. "Is it okay that we're still here? I'm walking Joey home today."

Mr. Sasko nods. "You bet it is. And guess what? I just got off the phone with Ms. Duxbury."

"You did?"

"Yep." He grins. "And she actually said that our grant application looks promising!"

"Promising?" I exclaim.

"That's right! That petition, plus the plan for the bathrooms and a promised donation of wood chips from the Burbanks, must have put it over the top."

"What does 'promising' mean?" asks Joey, the ball still tight in his hands. "Is it good?"

Mr. Sasko comes onto the blacktop. "It means I'm feeling pretty confident that we're okay for now. That the school is going to stay open."

"*Yay,*" Joey yells. "Now we really have to dunk the ball. To celebrate!"

I laugh and pick him up, and this time instead of his name, he's chanting: "Haycock School! Haycock School!"

⟨∾⟩

After Mr. Sasko has left, I turn to Joey. "You know what? Let's keep our celebration going. How about we stop at my house before I take you home. Maybe we can find ourselves a special snack."

"But I've never been to your house," Joey says.

I smile. "Then let's change that."

My mom looks up when we come through the door. She's got seed catalogs spread across the kitchen table. "Great news," I say. "Mr. Sasko thinks we're going to get the grant!"

"That's fantastic!" she says. "And, Joey—how nice to see you here!"

"Thanks, Mrs. Galenos," Joey says. "Your house is nice! Hey, my mom has the same teakettle!" He walks around the kitchen in a circle and then stops at the fridge. Joey looks at each one of the butterfly drawings in turn. "Who drew these?"

I exchange a look with my mom. I'm so glad we finally hung them up. "Alex did."

"They're great," Joey says. "I like how sparkly they are."

I nod. "And who drew that?" I point to the index card of bees that I hung next to the yellow butterfly at the very top of the fridge.

"I did!" Joey exclaims.

"It's awesome," I say. "And now I can see it every morning when I have breakfast."

"And the bees can hang out with the butterflies. Butterflies and bees make good friends, don't they?"

I smile. "They sure do."

Joey looks around. "So, what we gonna eat for a celebration?"

"You are in luck. I just made banana bread," my mom says.

"Ooh! I love banana bread," Joey says. "Yes, please! Do you always make banana bread? I want to come here every day! Then every day would be a celebration!"

My mom laughs as she starts stacking up her seed catalogs. "I promise to have banana bread for you anytime you want to stop by."

When Joey and I sit down to eat, I ask him, "So where'd

you get the idea to draw on an index card and then give it to someone?"

Joey shrugs. "I got a card that helped me, so I made you one, 'cause you were sick."

"You got an index card?"

Joey digs into his backpack. "Yeah, I keep it with me all the time. I found it next to the bench near the dentist's office after I had four cavities filled. Four!" He places the card on the table. It has a picture of a dandelion in front of mountains, and the words *You are amazing. And you are not alone!* written across the sky. All of it covered in glitter.

My breath catches in my throat. *Libby.*

Joey pats the card. "Finding it was the best part of my day."

Libby said she didn't know if anyone had gotten her cards, but Vincent had and Joey had. Still, without even knowing that, she kept putting them out into the world. Even when it was pouring rain.

Kept putting love into the world anyway.

"This is so cool," I tell Joey. "What do you say we make cards to send to someone else who needs cheering up?"

"Yeah!" he says.

I riffle through the desk in the kitchen until I find a stack of neon index cards and some markers. Joey whoops when I hold them up.

My mom pokes her head in. "You two sure are excited about something. You need any help?"

"You make one too," Joey shouts. "It's fun!" He picks up a bright-yellow index card and uncaps a black marker. "Now, who should we send them to?"

I look up at the glittery butterflies covering our fridge. "I think I know just the person."

LIBBY
THURSDAY, MAY 17

I'M CUTTING UP chicken thighs when my phone buzzes. I glance over, but I can't see it from here. It's probably my mom reminding me to be extra-careful with raw chicken. She didn't say anything about the index card on her windshield last night. I guess I should be glad she didn't light into me about how stupid it is to color with crayons.

And even though I hate cutting up chicken, because it's always cold and slimy, somehow I don't mind it as much today. Because if my mom's way of showing love is making sure I eat made-from-scratch meals, I know it's not easy to do that after a full day of work. But I wish she could understand that requiring "finely diced peppers" is more complicated than it needs to be. Once in a while, she could just give me a hug.

When I finish, I slide the chicken pieces into one of her baggies, wash my hands, and pour in the sauce so it can marinate in the fridge. Then I pick up the peppers. Maybe I could just chop them instead of finely dicing them. Would it really be so bad? Maybe I could ask her. I put the peppers back down and walk over to where my backpack is sitting on a kitchen chair, so I can dig out my cell phone.

But the text isn't from my mom. It's from Jack. And it has a picture of a kid with an enormous smile. And next to that smile is an index card that says: *You are amazing. And you are not alone!*

And suddenly I remember. That boy with the buzz cut outside the dentist's office. He got it!

His smile. I can't stop looking at it.

And those words on the index card! The words I wrote looking back at me now.

Are we amazing? Clearly.

Alone? Not him.

Not me either.

I'm still staring at the picture when another picture shows up. This time it's of a set of new index cards. Three of them. The message says:

Stamped and ready to go make someone else's day better.

All because of . . .

I cover my mouth and try to swallow the sob that's threatening to come out. It's like all the light from the sunrise is inside me, about to explode.

For me, I start texting my mom, the colored pencils and the index cards are things I use to help people feel better. I tap to add the photo of Joey. Sometimes a little can go a long way.

Then I add:

And I'm going to cut the peppers bigger this time. You can taste them more that way.

Because I realize: It doesn't matter how many times they ground me. Part of me is out there. In places I've never been. Affecting people I've never met. Making people smile like that. And there's no way they can stop it now. It's too big.

⟡

That night, when I go into my bedroom after brushing my teeth, there's something on my pillow. I let out a yelp. It's a brand-new set of colored pencils! And a pack of two hundred fifty index cards. Two hundred and fifty!

I grab them up to make sure they're real. They are.

There's no note, but that's okay. There's more than one way to tell someone they're loved.

I turn on the spot and head down the hall to find my mom. She's on the couch, watching one of her shows like she had nothing to do with this, but I know she did.

"Thank you," I say.

She waves me away. She's pretending she's too engrossed in the TV, but I see it. The corner of her mouth twitches into a smile. She reaches up, puts her hand gently on my head, and rests it there.

It isn't exactly a hug. But it's enough.

When I get back to my room, I throw all of Rex's dirty clothes in the closet and then sit down smack in the middle of my cleared-off floor. I rip open the packages and start in on the first index card. The Historic Mill Commemoration Day is just a few days away, with its softball game and walkways decorated with "historically accurate" pictures of old buildings. But when the fireworks go off that night, I won't need to be on anyone else's shoulders. Because my own two feet are rooted in the ground, and I'm blooming up and out into the world. As big and brilliant as any of those fireworks.

And if I have anything to do with it, those walkways are also going to be decorated with tons and tons of index cards filled with love.

T

MONDAY, MAY 21

I rub Peko's back as she sleeps.

Both of us are still full.

Vincent's sandwiches are good.

He should be here soon. His first geometry club meeting
was today.

I wait.

I want to hear how it went.

Maybe that's why it feels longer.

I wait more.

There. Someone's coming.

It's not Vincent.

It's the man who runs the church, the pastor.

He's coming over to me. Did I do something wrong? Are
they closing the drop-in center for this evening?

He has papers in his hand. Neon ones. Index cards?

"Are you T?" he says.

I nod.

He hands me an index card. "This is for you."

"What?" It's a postcard. The address says:

T
On the sidewalk near the Sunshine Center
511 10th Avenue East
Seattle, WA 98102

The stamp has a puffin on it.

"I don't understand," I say.

But the pastor just stands there calmly and waits.

I flip the card over. It says:

You are loved.

I look up at the pastor. "This can't be for me."

"You saw the address.

It is clearly for you.

And so is this one."

He hands me another.

"And this one."

I take them from him

Even though my hand has started to shake.

One has a picture of a bee drawn by a little kid.

The words *BEE yourself.*

The other has a drawing of a garden.
And a lot of words.
Sometimes even adults have growing to do . . .
What I'd give to go back in time and make sure my child knew I
loved him just as he was . . .

Something inside me
is shifting.

I look up at the pastor. "Can I use your phone?"

VINCENT
MONDAY, MAY 21

I CAN'T WAIT to tell T. I replay the conversation from geometry club at lunch in my mind as I walk. *Do you know the official word for a person who studies geometry?* the other student had whispered. *A geometer!* She said it like it was the most regal, magnificent thing on the planet. Her name is Penelope, and she loves triangles almost as much as I do.

Mr. Bond taught Penelope and me the coolest thing too. It turns out that a triangle doesn't only affect itself. If you extend out any of its sides, you suddenly have something called an exterior angle—which, I should note, looks suspiciously like the leg of a puffin extending from its webbed foot. And every change in the triangle results in a change to an exterior angle. And, of course, every change in an exterior angle affects the triangle.

I put my hands on my hips. It's all really simple once you see it. But that doesn't mean it'll ever stop being genius.

I come around the corner, and there's T.

But wait! Why is T standing up? Talking to that man?

T sees me and waves . . . and smiles?

When I get up close, I swear T's even taller than last time.

"Vincent," T says. "I'm going to make a phone call. Will you come with me?"

My mouth drops open. "Of course!"

"But first, you need to see something." T holds something neon out to me. Index cards. With addresses. Postcards.

And then I see where T is pointing.

They all have puffin stamps.

I stand up tall as I hand them back to T. "The puffins . . . ," I say, my voice cracking. "It was time for the puffins to reunite. No one should be alone in the open ocean forever."

T

MONDAY, MAY 21

Together we follow the pastor inside.
When I dial the number, my fingers shake,
but Vincent's standing next to me,
and the postcards are in my raincoat pocket.

"Hello?"
"Uncle Eddie, it's me."
There is a pause,
but then his voice is as thick as his cranberry sauce.
"I was hoping you'd call.
Where are you? We miss you!
Can I come get you?"

We talk for a while, and right before we hang up, my uncle
makes a sound that I've never heard him make before.
Like the squawk of a bird.

And I realize he's crying.
"I'm just so glad you're alive."

"Me too," I say.

I raise my eyes to see Vincent
forming a triangle with his hands.
He whispers,
"Me three."

I grin and then

put my hands on my hips
Vincent-style,
standing as a person
determined
to be exactly
who they are.

Because
I
am
me.

And
that
is awesome.

ACKNOWLEDGMENTS

THANK YOU TO Kara Lescord, whose beautiful determination to burst through concrete into sunlight sparked the seed that grew into this book.

Thank you to the women who provided me a sounding board as I tried to find a meaningful way to respond to hate back in December 2016. Those conversations led to the idea for the Local Love Brigade, a way for people to band together and send postcards filled with love to those facing hate. I am grateful to everyone in Vermont and across the country who started sending postcards . . . individuals, schools, faith groups, and others. Every time someone paused in their day to put their heart on a piece of paper and send it to a stranger, it moved me. And this book wouldn't exist without them.

Thank you to Karen Hesse. When I called her (shaking in my boots) to thank her for writing a blurb for my first book, she told me—quite forcefully—that I had to write another book.

"When are you going to write?" she asked.

"Early morning," I stammered.

"What are you going to say when friends invite you to breakfast?"

I swallowed. "I'll say, 'I can't, because Karen Hesse told me I can't.'"

Thank goodness for those early mornings.

Thank you to all of my young nonbinary friends and relatives who have demonstrated with grace how simple it is to be themselves. Thank you to those who read earlier versions of this story and offered feedback through a nonbinary lens, including Amber Leventry, Jude Anders, and Question Ricardo. Your insight was invaluable. And thank you to Krystale Chicoine, who once wrote *Impossible* on a Love Brigade postcard and then changed it to *I'm Possible*.

Thank you to All Pilgrims Christian Church, which served as a home away from home when I lived in the Capitol Hill neighborhood in Seattle as a young adult. And thank you to the drop-in center for homeless teens in its basement, where I worked to feed kids (and their pets) and where I learned about the determination and strength it takes to live on the street.

Thank you to my stepfather, Jim, for reminding me about the exterior angle theorem and for being the inspiration for the logical thumb-in-the-pie Uncle Eddie.

Thank you to my mom. Always. For everything. She really is right most of the time.

Thank you to the Rocket Cats, the greatest critique group ever. Jennifer Chambliss Bertman, Tara Dairman, and Elaine B. Vickers, you all are brilliant, and if there were a way to legally solidify our critique group as a permanent union, I would. Till death do us part.

Thank you to the other wonderful writers, educators, and all-around wise people who were willing to read this manuscript and help make it better: K. A. Holt, Jessica Lawson, Joy McCullough, Josephine Cameron, Kip Wilson, Kristin Crouch, and Kirsten Cappy.

Thank you to my agent, Tricia Lawrence, who believed in me and my career and was determined to find me a publishing house that could be my home.

Thank you to Nancy Paulsen for blowing my mind when she offered to publish this book and for exceeding my wildly high expectations of what it would be like to work with such a giant in the industry. Getting to be a collaborative partner with her and her editing genius is like running through a meadow at sunrise with your heart full to bursting—except that with Nancy there's no fear of ticks.

Thank you to the fabulous team at Penguin Random House, including Sara LaFleur, Elizabeth Johnson, and many more. And thank you to Chanelle Nibbelink, who created this book's glorious cover. It took my breath away, and I know Libby would love it too.

Finally, thank you to my husband, Dan, and my children, Ethan and Alice, who cheered me on through the writing of this—and through each of its many revisions. In all the world, there's nobody I'd rather quarantine with. May you fly free like fearless puffins in whatever direction your heart desires.